Vivienne Cleven was born in 1968 in Surat and grew up in western Queensland, homeland of her Aboriginal heritage. She left school at thirteen to work with her father as a jillaroo: building fences, mustering cattle, and working at various jobs on stations throughout Queensland and New South Wales.

In 2000, with the manuscript *Bitin' Back*, Vivienne entered and won the David Unaipon Award. In demand at literary events and workshops, she has published articles and fiction in anthologies, magazines and journals. Her second novel was *Her Sister's Eye*. Vivienne lives in the bush, is studying her PhD and is working on her latest novel.

First Nations Classics

BITIN' BACK

VIVIENNE CLEVEN

First published 2001 by University of Queensland Press
PO Box 6042, St Lucia, Queensland 4067 Australia
Reprinted 2005, 2010, 2012, 2017, 2021
This First Nations Classics edition published 2024

University of Queensland Press (UQP) acknowledges the Traditional Owners
and their custodianship of the lands on which UQP operates. We pay our
respects to their Ancestors and their descendants, who continue cultural and
spiritual connections to Country. We recognise their valuable contributions
to Australian and global society.

uqp.com.au
reception@uqp.com.au

Cover design by Jenna Lee
Typeset in 11.5/16 pt Bembo Std by Post Pre-press Group, Brisbane
Printed in Australia by McPherson's Printing Group

  First Nations Classics are assisted by
the Australian Government through
Creative Australia, its principal arts
investment and advisory body.

This project is supported by the Copyright Agency's Cultural Fund.

A catalogue record for this book is available from the National Library of Australia.

ISBN 978 0 7022 6851 9 (pbk)
ISBN 978 0 7022 6977 6 (epdf)
ISBN 978 0 7022 6978 3 (epub)

University of Queensland Press uses papers that are natural, renewable and
recyclable products made from wood grown in well-managed forests and other
controlled sources. The logging and manufacturing processes conform to the
environmental regulations of the country of origin.

MIX
Paper | Supporting
responsible forestry
FSC
www.fsc.org
FSC® C001695

For
My Family
Laura and Travis
Eddie Duncan
Jillian and Doreen Waud
Forever my heart

Contents

INTRODUCTION
by Melissa Lucashenko

First Nations narratives are many thousands of years old, but only in the past few decades have they become widely available to readers. The year 1988 saw the creation of the David Unaipon Prize, the first dedicated award for Indigenous authors in Australia. Twelve years later, the State Library of Queensland's black&write! program for First Nations literature was established. (Texan-born editor Sue Abbey was instrumental in both these important initiatives.) *Bitin' Back* won the David Unaipon Award in 2000. And when the inaugural black&write! editors-in-training were assigned five titles to study a decade later, two of those five titles – *Bitin' Back* and *Her Sister's Eye* – were by Kamilaroi author Vivienne Cleven.

The biography of the 2000 David Unaipon winner reads a bit like something out of Dickens. Born into stark poverty in the Queensland bush, Cleven was raised, like a lot of Aboriginal people in the 1960s, to expect a life of manual labour and poverty. Her family were no strangers to dirt floors nor to empty bellies. Schooling was intermittent, regularly interrupted by racism, poverty and transience. As a result Cleven left formal education at thirteen. Her life from then on was one of harsh physical labour on outback stations, building fences and doing stock work with her father. Not exactly a typical upbringing for a multi-award-winning Australian author in the late twentieth century. But an upbringing very much in keeping with the spirit of the David Unaipon Award founders, who sought to promote Indigenous authors who would otherwise struggle to be heard within the mainstream world of Australian publishing.

Very likely years of hard yakka in the dusty backblocks gave birth to the defining characteristic of Cleven's work: the intense vividness of her characters and their language. Her rural protagonists leap off the page fully formed, bursting with originality, energy and – sometimes – with anger. Black and white, they speak the unique patois of the country pub, the Aboriginal fringe camp and the cattle yard. Racism towards Aboriginal people in Cleven's work is not explained or debated. It's simply assumed, along with a host of other hard truths in an outback settlement that offers little more to its inhabitants than football, violence and poverty. Renowned Australian comedian HG Nelson has said that small Australian towns are places where 'you could murder someone and so long as you scored two tries on the weekend, you'd be sweet'. It's in just such a town, with exactly that ethos, that *Bitin' Back* is set.

The novel's protagonist, Aboriginal single parent Mavis Dooley, has many problems; her Kamilaroi son

Nevil instantly becomes the central one when he declares himself not a black football star but a white woman writer, and flat out asks to borrow one of his mother's dresses. Nevil has been smoking drugs, yes: 'The room smells like it's full a horseshit; Mary Jane floatin out the window.' But it's his sexual identity that really has Mavis worried. In a redneck town like theirs, appearing homosexual is asking for serious trouble, let alone cross-dressing. 'He's gone crazy n gay. A woman can't take it ... This here is dangerous business.' Horrified, Mavis just has time to comically bemoan that her black son didn't decide to be another kind of female author – an Aboriginal one: 'Someone spectable like Oodgeroo.' But Nevil insists he's not gay. He's simply a white female, and is to be addressed from now on as Miss Jean Rhys. When she realises he isn't joking, Mavis is at her wit's end to protect her apparently deranged boy from the Big Boys and Grunts of the local footy team, the Blackouts.

Uncle Booty reckons a spot of pig hunting will sort his nephew out: 'the boy's been watchin too much a that American shit on TV.' But Mave blames the absent father, Davo, 'friggin scourin off like that'. She attempts to lay down the law: 'Number one, Nevil, you're not a woman. Number two, ya not white. Number three, football is ya only way outta this town.'

Nevil ignores her and dons a red dress, only to be instantly crash-tackled by Uncle Booty and locked in his room for his own safety. 'I can't fight the bloody town for him,' the older man explains. The race is on to hide

Nevil/Jean from the homophobes and gossips of the town, as the big footy game gets ever closer.

Chaos ensues. A hapless white visitor from the big smoke is mistaken for a dangerous city drug dealer. Mavis's 'crazy-cracked' neighbour offers first Christianity and then firearms to fend off disaster. Nevil's bewildered girlfriend reports him missing, involving the police in the whole affair. Mavis's desperation to hide Nevil's deviance culminates in a siege in her own home. And even the cop who arrests her afterwards wants to know if Nevil is 'ready for the big game'.

For all its comic energy, violence is omnipresent in *Bitin' Back*. This is most obvious in the ongoing threat to Nevil's life if his alter ego is exposed. But Nevil's Aboriginal girlfriend Gracie does get seriously bashed – by police at a nearby land rights demonstration. The Aboriginal men's lives revolve around pig hunting, illegal bare-knuckle boxing and, of course, footy. Mavis herself flies into a rage and beats up Darryl, a local who's about to kick her only friend, Gwen, in a pub fight. Verbal abuse is rampant between the black and white women too. This brutality, simmering permanently just below the surface of Mavis's life and regularly erupting above it, is never questioned by her. It's just the way things are. Imagine *Wake in Fright*, but the calls are coming from inside the house – forever.

Bitin' Back was well ahead of its time. *Priscilla, Queen of the Desert* showed queers on a road trip to Uluru – but those queers were from Sydney, not trapped living cheek-by-jowl in a tiny place with those who hated their very existence. Even after a successful referendum for marriage equality, it remains difficult for many queer Australians to come out. This is doubly so in the often blatantly homophobic towns west of the Great Dividing Range. Mavis is in equal parts horrified by, and fearful for, her 'gay' son, even after he makes it clear he isn't in fact gay. Questions of trans identity, unheard of by the Australian mainstream in 2000, are briefly posed by Cleven. 'Boot, do ya reckon Nev was meant to be born a girl? Like … um … he's got too much woman in him stead a man? Like he's a bit man n mostly woman?'

In 2023 this question might have been given a very different exploration. However, we come to understand by the end of the novel that *Bitin' Back* is only superficially about gender or sexuality. Cleven has penned a raw and honest portrait of rural Queensland at the turn of the century. On one level the narrative is about the perils of being queer, yes. On another it can be read as being about anyone visibly different in a stiflingly conformist town determined to enforce its conformity with violence. As Mavis tells her friend Gwen about the gossips who torment her: 'Yep, that's the nature a this town, making yarns, tearin some poor bastard to pieces!'

Happily, 'ol black-arse Mavis' prevails, thanks to her wit and courage. And, similarly, writing out of a bush culture where 'a woman's got to be as tough as a man, but not show it', Cleven has bestowed on Australian literature a gift of gritty Blak realism that is as funny as it is forthright. The reissuing of *Bitin' Back* should lead to a new wave of readers for this brilliant yet little-known Murri author.

Bullfight critics row on row
Crowd the vast arena full
But only one man is there who knows
And he's the man who fights the bull

Anonymous

1

Jean Arrives

The boy is curled up in his bed like a skinny black question mark. Ain't like he got a lot of time to be layin bout. A woman gotta keep him on his toes. That's me job; to keep the boy goin. Hard but, bein a single mother n all. Be all right if the boy had a father. Arhhh, a woman thinks a lot a shit, eh? A woman's thoughts get mighty womba sometimes!

I pinch me nose closed; the room stink like it been locked up for years. I shake Nevil awake. 'Nev. Nevil, love. Come on wake up. Ya got a interview today, down at the dole office.'

'Wha … what?' He rolls over, the sheet twisted round his sweat-soaked body. He rubs his eyes and looks up at me with sleepy confusion.

'The dole office. Interview. Ya know, today. In bout thirty minutes. Come on, no use layin there like a leech.'

'Who, what?' He struggles up on his bony elbows, givin me a sour gape of bewilderment. *The boy look myall this mornin.*

'On ya bloody feet. Don't want none a ya tomfoolery

today.' I look at the beer bottles, the bong and all them books scattered on the floor. I eyeball the titles – *Better Sex, How to Channel Shakespeare, Oscar Wilde, Ernest Hemingway. Yep, was always a mad one for readin, our Nev.*

I turn round. He's still in bed, his arms folded behind his head as he stares up at the ceiling. 'Jesus Christ! Get outta friggin bed will ya! A woman got better things to do than piss bout here all day whit you! Come on, Nevie, love.' I soften me voice to a low crawly tone. 'Mum's got bingo. Might hit the jackpot, eh?'

'Who's Nevil?' he asks, starin down at his hairy, mole-flecked arms.

'Wha …? What's wrong whit ya? Ya sick?' I peer at his face.

'I'm not sick. And don't call me Nevil!' He nods his head and his bottom lip drops over, like he's gonna bawlbaby.

'Yeah, if you're not Nevil then call me a white woman!' I sit on the edge of his bed, laughter bubblin in the back of me throat. *Was always a joker, our Nev.*

'I'm not Nevil, whoever that is!' He busts his gut in sudden anger, his hands curled into fists.

'Talk shit,' I say, waitin for the punchline.

'How dare you talk to me like that!' His voice sounds like he really true means it as he glares sharp eye at me.

'I'll speak to ya any friggin way I wanna! Now get outta bed before I kick that black arse of yours!' I stand up, me hands on me hips, foot tappin the floorboards. *Don't push me, Sonny Boy.*

He pulls the sheet up to his face, his brown eyes peepin out from the cover. 'Call me Jean,' he whispers.

'Jean! Jean!' The laughter jump out, I double over holdin onto me gut, heehawin and gaspin for breath. 'Yeah, good one Nev, bloody funny.' I take control of meself when I suddenly realise how still and quiet he is. *Not like Nevie.*

'Call me Jean – Jean Rhys, that's my real name,' he says, droppin the sheet, showin his thick black chest hair.

'What the fuck …! Are you on drugs, son? Hard shit, eh?' I peer at his face, waitin for a confession. *The boy flyin high or what?*

'Nope. Just call me Jean.'

'Jean. Right, I get the joke, ha, ha, funny,' I say, takin a closer look at him but seeing nothin outta the ordinary.

'It's not funny! I can't see any humour in my name. How would you like me to make fun of you, huh?'

I walk over to the bed. 'Somethin real wrong whit ya, Nev?' I drop me eyeballs down at him. *Too much smokin pot n pissin up all that grog is what does it. How the friggin hell did he come up with a cock-a-doodle name like Jean Reece, for God's sake! A woman's name!*

'Just remember I'm Jean Rhys, the famous writer,' he says, flashin his chompers as he picks at his nails. As though to say: 'Are you madfucked, Ma? Can't ya see who I am?'

'A writer! A woman writer! Jesus Christ Almighty! Next you be tellin me yer white!' Me hand flies to me chest, as though to stop me thumpin heart. *Weedeatin, that's what's wrong whit him. Yarndi messin whit his scone.*

3

'Yep, sure am,' he answers, throwin his legs over the side of the bed.

'Nevil, stop this rot! You startin to worry poor ol mum here, son. Anythin you wanna talk bout? Girlfriends, football, yarndi?' *Sometime talkin help clean out the shit.*

'Nope. Sure appreciate if you'd call me by my right name though,' he says, one hand scratchin his arse, the other rubbin his stubbly chin.

'Okay, Nevil. Nevil Arthur Dooley, male, twenty-one years old, black fella from the bush.' I give the boy a smooth n oily smile. *Gotcha! Take that one!*

'Damn you! It's Jean, Jean Reece! J-E-A-N! R-H-Y-S! Get it!' he yells. Spit flies across the room and lands on me face.

'Oh righto, Jean. Is it miss or missus?' I decide to go along with him, to play out this little joke. *Jean Rhys, eh. Biggest load a goona a woman doned ever heard.*

'*Miss'll* do fine, thank you, Mum.' He smiles, then drops his head n looks down at the rubbish-strewn floor.

'Well, Miss Jean Rhys, what may I ask have you got in those undies there, huh?' I throw him a spinner. *Take the bait, boy. Our Nev n his jokes. A regular commeediann.*

'That's crass. What do you think's in there?' He spins round, grabs the bath towel off the window ledge and winds it round his skinny hips.

'Well ... I really don't know any more.'

'Hmmpph, stupid question, Mother. Now where are my clothes?' he asks in a pissy sorta way, runnin his tongue cross his thick-set lips as he catches a glance at hisself in the mirror.

'In the wash, Nevil – I mean Jean.' I walk over and stand behind him as he stares at hisself.

'Have you ever seen such bewdiful hair, huh?' he says, his fingers tryin to comb through the baby arse fluff on top of his scone.

'Yeah,' I whisper, by this time knowin somethin is very wrong whit me only kid.

I catch his eyes and look into them, wonderin what mischief lays there. I see nothin. His eyes hold no deep secrets. I reach out and touch his shoulder. 'Tell Mum, Nevil, tell Mum.' I will him to answer me, to tell me somethin has happened, someone has paid him to pull this stuntin on me. *Ain't like Nev to be arsin bout like this. Talkin mad, sorta like he got that possessin stuff. A manwomanmanwoman. Like the boy mixin his real self up whit another person.*

'I need a frock. A nice one,' he says, pullin faces at hisself.

'A frock! Sweet Jesus, Nev, come on, love!' I take a wonky step back from him, feelin like as though he's done punched me in the gut. *The boy is deadly serious.*

'You heard me. I can't very well get about in those things there, can I?' He points to a pile of dirty jeans.

'You have before.' I try to smooth him over, 'I can get a fresh pair off the line if ya want.' I feel somethin grip me like death as I try to imagine me big-muscled, tall hairy son walkin round the town in a dress.

5

The shock brings vomit up to sit at the back of me throat. I realise with a sick despair that he means to wear a dress right or wrong. *He won't back out even for me. He's mad in the head. He's gone crazy n gay. A woman can't take it.*

Now let me see, yeah, I member that ol girl long time past, this sorta thing happened to her. It make a woman wonder: ya got black fellas sayin they white. Ya got white fellas sayin they black. I just dunno what's racin round in they heads. Cos, when ya black, well, things get a bit tricky like. See now, if ya got a white fella then paint him up black n let the man loose on the world I reckon he won't last long. Yep, be fucked from go. But when ya got a black fella sayin he's a woman – a white woman at that! Well, the ol dice just rolls n another direction. Ain't no one gonna let the man ... boy, get away whit that! This here is dangerous business.

'Well ... I spose ... you'll ... fit into a dress a mine. Tell me, what's Gracie gonna think, eh?' I shake me head at him, the idea comin to me as I speak. 'She won't like it, Gracie girl, havin a boyfriend walkin bout in women's clothes. She won't put up whit it. She'll leave fer sure!' I let it all out, jabbin the air whit me finger.

'Well, too bad ain't it. Anyway, who's Gracie?' Nev turns round to face me.

'Don't talk stupid. Gracie's your girlfriend. Enough of this for once and all. I gotta go to bingo, the others'll be waitin for me. So get dressed; hurry up.'

He walks towards the bathroom, heavin his shoulders up and down as he sighs and mumbles to himself. There's somethin wrong whit the way he walks, steppin ballerina like as he goes down the hallway. Suddenly I wonder if our Nev is one a those.

One of em homos. Well, they don't call em that any more. Gay, that's the word people use. Jesus Christ! Can ya wake up gay? Must do, Nevil did. But then again some people can con theyselves that they anythin. Thinkin of that ol girl, what was her name? It were Phyllis, Phyllis Swan. If a woman's recollection is right, she were parted from her own mob by em government wankers; they reckon she too white for the others, eh. Too white, load a goona. When she growed up a bit more her skin turned up real charcoal like. Yeah, she coloured into a piece a coal. Black as Harry's arse. The wankers say: she too black for us, send the girl back. So back she go to her mob. They didn't want her. The whites didn't want her. She was sorta stuck in the middle like. Piggy in de middle.

Now what she doned?

Oh yeah, she done tell everyone that she's not Phyllis Swan at all! Oowhhh noooo! She says she really the Queen a England! Conned herself good n proper. The mad thing was, white fellas treated the woman whit respect! Like she truly were the Queen! I swear to God every time I seed that woman she were gettin whiter every day! White as friggin frost. Like she believed it so much that her skin was believin it too! Funny sorta turnout n all. Maybe this somethin like Nevil goin through. Conned hisself good n proper like. Hope he don't start thinkin that he be the friggin Queen! Jeeessuuss.

Now, how I'll tell me brother Booty? He won't like it! He'll kick Nev's arse for sure. Oh geez, what's a woman to do? It's all Davo's fault. Yep, pissin off on the boy just like that. No father

7

to play football whit, play cricket whit, nothin. *Spose a woman'll have to try n get Booty to have a yarn to him. Me boy won't listen to me. Now where the friggin hell did he get a name like Jean Rhys? A white woman writer, geez, couldn't he a picked a black woman writer? Someone spectable like Oodgeroo? Bloody white woman me fat arse!*

That's our Nev's problem, got his head stuck in all em books. Brainwashed. Them books have brainwashed him. Yeah, reckon that's bout the strength of it. Ain't no kid ever woked up whit headcrackin shit like this.

I let me thoughts go while I radar Nev's bedroom, lookin for any sign – any *gay* sign. In the corner books sit stacked up on each other, some tattered and dog-eared, others brand new. *Well, spose he does spend his money on other things part from piss n dope.*

I kneel down and look closer at the cover pictures and titles. *Yeah, some freaky stuff here all right.* I look for anythin that might have the name Jean R-h-y-s. Unstackin the books, I run me eyes over each one. There must be somethin here. Some clue.

Then I do notice somethin, five books by the same writer. *An Ideal Husband, Salome, The Importance of Being Earnest, Lady Windermere's Fan, A Woman of No Importance.* I take in the writer's name: Oscar Wilde. A playwright, the cover says. *What the hell's a playwright?*

I flick the cover open but there seems nothin outta place, nothin that would brainwash a man into thinkin hisself a woman. Just writin. Me eyes flick back to the other book, *A Woman of No Importance. Now that sounds a bit suss. Maybe the boy don't think he important? A Woman of No Importance? Hhhmmm.*

Sighin, I get up to me feet decidin I've had enough of this Nevil wantin to be a woman shit. *There's only one person who can talk some sense into the boy and I'll have to go and find him. Yep, can't have Nevil walkin down the main street in a dress. Geez.*

I walk past the bathroom. Nevil's voice sings out loud and deep. 'I am woman, hear me roar!'

'Bloody wake up to yerself, Nevil!' I yell as I open the front door and step out onto the street. *Watch me roar, Jeesus Christ! What's he now, a lion?*

'He woke up like that.' I look at Booty from across the kitchen table.

'Mave, men don't wake up bein poofters. Look at me, you don't see me wantin to wear women's clothes, eh?' He sips his beer.

'I'm tellin ya, Booty, he wasn't like that yesterday. He wake up like that! Sorta like … um, whatever it is, just stayed hidin in him n jumped out this morning,' I say, flappin me arms out to prove me point.

'Jumped out, my black arse. He was always like that, Mave, you jus never saw it is all. Women's clothes, Jesus!' Booty shakes his head, disgust washin over his fat face.

'Yeah, what bout Gracie, eh? Tell me that?'

'A cover. He's just using her as a cover. Ya hear bout all these movie stars n such, tellin the world they're queer.

"Comin outta the closet", they call it. Yep, I seen all that sorta shit on Ricki Lake. Women wantin to be men and men wantin to be girls. Yeah, Mave, the boy's been watchin too much a that American shit on TV. Seems to a man that kids don't know who they are. They all wussies I reckon. Black wantin to be white; white wantin to be black. That's where all these ideas come from – TV. Like he shamed a who he is or somethin.'

'Booty, he don't hardly watch TV. Nope, all he does is read them books a his. It's them books puttin ideas into his head. Brainwashin him, Booty.' I slump me shoulders wearily.

'Well, what can a man do, eh? He won't listen to his ol uncle here.' Booty gets up from his chair and walks over to the window, shrugging his broad shoulders.

'Yeah, but it's not only that. He thinks he's a writer! A white woman writer. Thinks his name is Rhys!'

'What the ...?' Booty croaks, swinging round on his heels, mouth agape, a stunned look on his dial.

'Jean Rhys. J-e-a-n R-h-y-s. That's his new name, so he reckons. She sposed to be a writer. Can't say I heard a the woman. Don't read books meself. Must go n ask Lizzy at the library there. She'd know bout this woman, I betcha.'

I watch Booty's face turn a faint shade of grey, the veins stickin out on his thick neck. 'What the hell's wrong with that boy! Jean Rhys, eh. He needs a good throttlin, that's what he needs. And I'm just the man to do it! Ain't no bloody nephew a mine gonna go dancin round the town callin hisself a woman!'

Booty busts his guts, pullin out a chair with such force that the can a beer topples to the floor.

'Righto, don't go givin yerself a heart condition, Brother. All I'm askin is for you to have a good talk to him. I blame it on Davo. The way he upped and pissed off on us. That's half the trouble, I betcha,' I say, feelin me heart start to gallop as the memory of Davo comes back. *Davo, friggin scourin off like that. No wonder Nev don't know hisself.*

'Bullshit! Never worried him all these years. Why would it worry him now? Nah, the boy's got a screw loose upstairs. Only thing you can do is get him to Doctor Chin. Take a good look at that head a his. I heard a people doin some sicko things – but this! Well, this really is somethin. Bad, fuckin bad business.' Booty gives me a serious, this-is-gone-too-far look.

'Maybe yer right. Can you come over n talk to him first? See, I'm thinkin he'll listen to you.'

'Righto, Mave. Gotta stop him from gettin outside in that friggin frock. Imagine his mates n the others, specially the footy team! They'd tear him to pieces for sure! You know what this town's like, Mave. They'd pick him to death.' Booty gets to his feet. 'Ready?'

'Yeah. But I'll warn ya, it's not a pretty sight. When I left him he was singin in the bathroom bout bein a woman n roarin.' I shake me head, me own words seem unreal to me own ears.

Booty strides out in front of me. Each step he takes drives into the footpath. His shoulders hunch forward as

11

though he's ready to tackle somebody, ready to put em into the ground.

Up at the corner shop I notice Big Boy Hinch, one of Nev's mates from the Blackouts, our local footy team. I silently pray he don't ask bout Nev.

'Hey there, Missus Dooley. Where's the Nev?' he asks the dreaded question as he shoves potato chips into his big mouth.

'Nev. Well … um … he's crook. Got a flu or somethin,' I answer, watchin the way his muscley arms ripple.

'He's crook, eh. A man'll have to get him back onto that football field, best thing for him. We got the game comin up with the Rammers next week. Hope he's right for that. Best player we got, Nev.' Big Boy smiles, football pride drippin from his eyes.

'That's our Nev. Now look, you tell em other fellas not to call round my place. Nev needs a good rest. He'll be right by next week I reckon.' I give him a wide smile, wonderin what he'd do if he saw our Nev this mornin, singin n dancin round. *Hmmph, probably tear him a new arsehole.*

'Mave! Come on, woman!' Booty yells out from the end of the street.

'Comin! Righto, Big Boy, see ya, love.'

'See ya at the game, Missus Dooley.'

'Dunno bout that,' I whisper, trottin down the road.

★

Nevil sits on the edge of his bed, a book in one hand, a beer in the other. A joint hangin outta his slack gob. The room smells like it's full a horseshit; Mary Jane floatin out the window.

'Nev, Uncle's here to see ya.' I notice the way his legs are crossed over each other like one of em Buddah people. He ignores me. 'Nev love, lovey, Uncle Booty's waitin in the kitchen for ya.'

'What? Who?' he asks, bringin his head up to gaze at me with bloodshot eyes.

'Uncle. He's here right now.'

'Why?' He takes a drag.

'To talk. Um … he was just goin by, wanted to see ya is all.' I take a step into the room.

'Is this about Jean, eh? Cos if it is then I'm not talking to anyone,' he answers.

'Jean? Who's Jean?' I try.

'Don't start this again, *Mother*. You know very well who Jean is.' A touch of anger to his voice.

'Oh yeah, I *forgot*.' I give him a sour I've-had-enough-of-you look. 'Nevil, what is that on your face?' I peer at him.

'Nothing much.' He reaches over and stubs out the smoke.

'*Make-up*? Nevil Dooley, is that woman paint on that face a yours!' I walk right into the room.

'So? And don't call me Nevil!' He's all pissed off n riled like.

'It's make-up! Where the hell did you get that!' I slit me eyes at him. *Face paint. Clown colourin.*

13

'Oh, somewhere.' He takes a sip of beer.

'Nevil Dooley! What the hell's goin on here, Sonny Jim!' I turn to the doorway. Booty blocks the exit with his large frame, his hands on his hips as he glares in at Nevil.

'Hello, Uncle. I ain't doing nothing.' Nevil gives him a wide, yarndi grin.

'Son, what the fuck is that on ya face?' Booty strides into the room, gut swingin from side to side, eyes narrowed and mouth twisted. *He gonna take a hunk a flesh.*

'Lipstick, eyeshadow, eyeliner. Reckon it looks okay?' Nevil uncurls his legs, arches his eyebrows, puckers his mouth.

'Look here, son, you can't go gettin bout like that! What are ya, a fuckin woman!' Booty tightens his mouth, a small quiver shaking his frame.

'My business. I'm not hurting anyone, am I?' Nevil reaches down by the bed and picks up a small floral-print bag.

'You got this shit from TV, didn't ya? Watchin too much American sicko shit, eh? Ricki Lake, is that it?' Booty yells, his fat arms choppin the air.

'Nope. I'm Jean Rhys, in case Mother hasn't already told you.' Nevil pulls out a tube of lipstick. 'Seductive Pink' is written large and posh like on the side a it.

'Shit. Bullshit! You a poofter now, son?' Booty walks to the edge of the bed, shoulders hunched, ready to fly.

'Don't be stupid. What's wrong with people in this house? It's as though a girl's committed some heinous

14

offence, like murdered someone or something.' Nevil puckers up his mouth an smears lipstick cross his tyre-tread lips.

'That's it! That's it!' Booty explodes; sweat poppin out on his forehead, his veins stickin up like they ready to jump outta the man's arms as he grabs Nevil by the singlet. 'Fucken ratbag! What's got into ya? Causin ya mother all this grief! Now get into that bathroom an take that shit off ya face!' Booty shakes a crunched fist in Nevil's face.

'Leave me alone, leave me alone,' Nevil bawlbaby.

'Now you cut this crap out, son. And lay off the fuckin drugs too. Your heads fucked enough already.' Booty pulls Nevil up to his wonky feet.

'Listen to your uncle, Nev, he knows best,' I say softly.

'Yeah, yeah. Let go of me, Uncle,' whisperin weak, Nevil looks up into Booty's angry sweat slicked dial.

'Fucken no more a this shit, Nevil! Ya gotta pull that head a yours in, right?'

'Hmm, yeah, spose.' But Nevil's voice don't sound like he means it. 'Anyway, I gotta go to the dole office. So you can leave now, I gotta get dressed.'

'Now, Sonny, if ya wanna have a man talk or somethin, come over ta me.' Booty pauses for a minute then says, 'But if ya gonna be keepin on at this shit, then a man's gonna have to settle ya down, n pretty fucken soon.' He wrinkles his brow, his bottom lip twitchin.

'Yeah, yeah, okay Uncle.'

15

'Right then, that's that. How bout a cup a tea, Mave?' Booty asks over his shoulder as he leaves the room.

'Righto.' I look behind me. *That'll sort him over. That was all the boy needed, a good yarnin to.*

Back in the kitchen Booty pulls out a chair. 'Reckon he's right now or what?'

'Dunno, spose so,' I reply, feeling sick in me gut, but hopeful.

'Geez, you weren't wrong bout him. Where the hell did he come up whit this shit?' Booty drops his eyebrows as he looks my way, his fingers tap tappin on the table.

'I dunno ya tell me. Those books gotta lot to do whit it, I reckon,' I answer, pouring the tea.

'Ain't like he had any sort of buse. You know, bashin kids so they wind up bein pissed up in they heads. Nah, ain't like he was brought up like that, eh Mave?' Booty nods and takes a sip a tea.

'No, Boot. Never had a hard life like us fellas. Wouldn't know what it's like to be so hungry you'd eat a dead horse. Nah, whatever it was it comed on him just like that. Sorta like some nightmare he can't get out of.' I sigh and then this thought comes to me sudden like. 'Boot, do ya reckon Nev was meant to be born a girl? Like … um … he's got too much woman in him stead a man? Like he's a bit man n mostly woman?'

'A sheila! Jesus, Mave! The boy's got nuts, for cryin out loud! The only half woman he's got is up there in that mad head a his!' Booty's stomach shakes the table as he splutters and gasps, laughin loudly.

'Orh. Well …' I stop as I hear a small sound in the hallway. I turn round in my chair. 'Jesus Christ!' I stifle a scream in me throat as I gawk at the sight before me. Nevil slides long the hall, frocked in me bright red dress, his face covered in make-up, on his feet a pair of dirty, fallin-apart sandshoes. He grins idiot-like as he stares back at me, holdin tight a handbag to his chest.

'Hey, Mum,' he mouths, creepin, his back gainst the wall.

Booty jumps up to his feet. 'Done fuckin told ya!' he roars. As fast as his big body can move he rushes forward and tackles Nevil, gut-section, bringin him to his knees.

'Mum, Mum, get him off!' Nevil squeals, hittin Booty on the back whit his handbag.

'Help me, Mave! Get him to his room!' Booty shouts, holdin Nevil's arms to his sides.

I stand up on shaky legs, uncertain as what to do. Then Booty pulls Nevil up by the dress and shoves him down the hallway.

'Let go! Let me go! Jesus, Uncle, let me go!' Nevil's voice cracks like a teenage girl as he struggles.

'Can't do that, Sonny Jim!' Booty growls.

I run up behind them and watch as Booty throws Nevil into his room and slams the door.

'Have you got a key?' he gasps.

'Yeah, I have. What ya gonna do, Booty?' A sick sussin grips me.

'Lock him in. Can't have him goin down the street like that, can we? Jeez, Mave, what'll the town think?'

I hesitate for a moment. 'Um … yeah, all right,' I answer, handing over the door key, but not liking the idea at all.

After Booty locks the door Nevil starts screaming from the room, so loud that I can only hope me neighbour, Missus Warby, don't call the boys in blue.

'Let him sweat it out. Don't worry, Sis, he'll come out of it. We just have to wait is all.' Booty puts a hand on me shoulder.

'It's not right, Booty, is it? Lockin a grown man in his room.' I feel guilty, sick at heart.

'No, it's not, Mave. But it's for his own good. They'd kick the shit outta him out there on the street.'

'Yeah, yeah, I know. But I think Nev can handle hisself pretty good when he wanna.' *I can only hope.*

'That's not the point, Sis, they'd mob him, ya know that.' Booty looks tired out, slumpin his shoulders forward. 'Mave, I can't fight the bloody town for him.'

'Yeah, Brother, true. Well, I'll see what he's like this arvie, eh?'

'No, leave him in there. Maybe he'll wake up tamarra n be back to hisself. Wait and see what happens,' Booty throws over his shoulder as he goes out the front door.

Going into the kitchen I hear Nev singin, this time bout being a lost soul or somethin. I sit at the table, drop me head into me hands and think back, tryin to find some clue as to where this all began.

2

Missin

Gracie's face creases into a map of worry lines. 'Haven't seen him since yesterday, Mum. I'm startin to wonder what happened to him.' Tears gather at the corners of her eyes.

'Gracie, love, don't you worry, he'll be right. Ya know our Nevie, just ups n offs, don't worry bout no one but hisself.' I turn away from her, the lies sittin uneasy on me tongue.

'Are you sure he never said where he was goin?'

'I reckon he'll be home tamarra. Now stop all this worryin, ain't no good for ya.'

'Another woman. That's it. He's got another sheila, hasn't he?' she asks, lips puckered, her watery brown eyes screwed into mean slits.

'Oh, come on, love. Nev's faithful. Ain't no other woman. He just needed to, um … find a friend a his.' Another lie forces its way out smooth like.

'Mum, you'd tell me, wouldn't ya?' she asks, a suss sneer washin over her dial.

'Yeah, of cour—' I stop. Sounds of singin are comin

from Nevil's bedroom. I stand rooted to the spot, me shoulders tense. *Here we go.*

Gracie cocks her ear towards the noise. 'What's that? Sounds like a woman singin?'

'Oh, that's Missus Warby, the lonely ol piece next door.' I smile weakly. 'Well, love, I've gotta go to bingo now. See ya some other time, eh?' I grab her arm and push her towards the door. *Gotta get the girl out.*

'Oh, right. Well … tell Nev I was here, okay?' She throws a suss look past me shoulder. *Like she knows.*

'Sure will.' I watch her as she walks down the street, then I turn round and start back into the house when I hear: 'Missus Dooley, Missus Dooley!'

I glance up towards the street corner and see Big Boy n another fella joggin along passin a football as they come towards me.

'Hey there, whatcha up to, Big Boy?' I smile at him, eyein the dirty black and orange guernsey he wears. *I wonder if the boy ever changes it. He smells like piss n ol sweat.*

'This here's Grunt. Grunta the Punter, down here for the match next week.' Big Boy motions to his friend.

'How ya doin, Grunt? Reckon yous'll win the match?' I watch the way he flexes his arm muscles as he jogs on the spot.

'Yep. See, they got ol Grunt down here cos these mob a wussies'll get whipped whitout me.' His pockmarked face creases up into a toothless smile.

'Talkin outta ya arse!' Big Boy nudges him in the ribs,

20

then looks shameface. 'Ooh, gee, sorry, Missus Dooley, a man forgot hisself there.'

'Woman's heard worser than that. Anyway, who's the coach this time round?' I'm tryin to put off the sure-as-shit question bout Nev, as I edge inside the house.

Big Boy answers. 'George. George Spiros – you know, the old Greek dude owns the pub. Well, he only just bought it. You seen em yet? Him n his mob? Geez, he got some daughters.'

'Daughters, eh. Nope, ain't seen em.'

'Yeah, well, we lookin for the Nev. Can I go n see him or what?' Big Boy's got one foot jammed in the doorway.

'Oh no, love, Nev's really crook n ya might catch that flu thing off him. Wouldn't be no good for the whole team to come down whit it, eh?' I shake me head vigorous like, purse me lips and drop me shoulders to let him know I'm deadly serious.

'Shit! Never knewed it were that bad!' Big Boy takes a quick step back as though the house itself has some poxy disease.

'Yeah, that's right. Be shame if youse couldn't play cos ya got it too. Nah, Nev'll get over it pretty soon.' *Can only hope.*

'What sorta flu?' Grunt questions, his arms crossed.

'Well, I … I don't rightly know. But a bad one! Yeah, real bad. Like it make him delirium n all, see.' I look at the geranium bush near the corner of the house. *I don't like the way that boy lookin at me. Like he know I'm lyin.*

21

That's the problem whit tellin big ones – ya jus dunno who gonna be sussin on ya.

'I had somethin like that. I ain't heard a no flu makin a man delirious but.'

'This one's different. It's a … a … Geranium's Palsy flu!' I throw out. *Now where the hell a woman get that from! Geranium Palsy, geez.*

'Orh, that sounds real rugged.' Big Boy's face screws up like he doned shit his pants or somethin. *He looks disgusted.*

'Sure is, son. Anyway, I gotta go down to bingo. Ya want me to tell Nev anything?' I hold the edge of the door, ready to slam it shut right in the boy's face.

'Yeah, tell him he'd better get on his feet soon. The other fellas are startin to worry bout him not bein able to play at all.'

'Doncha worry, Nev'll be right for the game.' I look at both of em. For a fraction of a second I wonder what they'd do if I told em the news Nev's in the bedroom wearin women's clothes and make-up all over his face. Yeah, n he thinks he's a woman writer called Jean Rhys. I almost burst into laughter at the thought.

'Right then, Missus Dooley. Thanks anyway.' Big Boy waves as he goes out the gate. I watch em as they amble back down the street. Two solid footballers, all muscle, all man. *Why couldn't Nev be like those normal boys? Jus havin a normal life playin football n worryin bout girls? Nah, not our Nev! Oowhh nnoo, have to be a friggin woman.*

I turn and go back inside, slammin the door behind me. I put the kettle on the stove and sit down. Cockin me ear towards Nev's room I hear no noises, no singin or screamin. Thinkin bout him locked in there makes a woman feel like a ton a shit. *I mean he's not a kid is he, Mavis Dooley? He's a grown man. Go down n let him out. Gorn, gorn.* I jump off the chair and go down to his room.

'Nev, love. Nev, ya awake?' I put the key in the latch and turn it. Then I hear a clatterin comin from behind the door. The same clatter I've heard many times before. *Clickclackclickclack ... now what that noise is?* I push open the door and take a swift step inside.

'Nev, love, are ya shitty whit ol mum?' I use my best crawlin voice. *Course he shitty. Whatcha think. Locked away like some sorta mad animal.*

'Don't call me Nevil! And don't barge in like that, Mother,' he growls.

'Sorry, Son, I ... um. Want Mum to get ya a feed?' I offer in a con type a voice.

'I'm right. Anyway, I'm not hungry,' he snaps.

I move closer into the room. He sits up on the pillows. There's a typewriter beside the bed and papers scattered all over the room.

He still wears the make-up and the dress but he look ragged-worn and pissed out. I notice the beer on the floor, a half-opened carton of tall necks.

'Love are you drinkin those hot?'

'Yeah. Unless you want to let me out of this room so I can put them in the fridge. Is Booty gone?'

'Yep. But he said you gotta behave otherwise he'll be back.'

'Ain't done nothing wrong,' he sulks.

'Son, what ya doin whit all that paper n stuff?'

'Nothing. Don't ask, you wouldn't understand,' he whines back.

'Oh, like that is it? Can't tell ya own mother anythin now?' I sit down on the floor and stare at him. *Friggin kids.*

'There's no use, is there? Wouldn't matter, Ma, you just – ahh, never mind.' He shakes his head.

'Hmm, not gonna tell Mum, eh?'

'Ain't nothin for you to worry about.'

'Big Boy and Grunt, a new player up from Currajong Creek, was here. Lookin for ya to go to the trainin for the game next week. Ya goin?' I watch a flicker of somethin cross his face.

'Football, well … gee, I don't know any more, Mum. It's like that's all they know around here.' He turns his face to the window.

'Nev, I thought ya loved footy. They sure need ya on that game, so Big Boy reckons.'

'Yeah, I love footy, Ma. But shit, there's other things to do in life, aren't there?' He sounds real serious.

'Spose ya got a point there. Well, are ya playin or not? I don't want em mob comin here askin all sorts a things.'

'I don't know. Yeah, I will,' he says, holdin up a piece a paper and starin at it. 'Mum, do something for me, *pleease.*'

'Yeah, what?' I ask, suss, not liking the con job tone of his voice.

'Just call me Jean, okay?' He looks across at me, his face bolted serious like.

'If that's what ya want. But, look, Nev, if ya got a boyfriend ya can tell ol Mum here.' I offer me best see-I-understand-many-things look. *But I'm not standin nothin. Homo – gay – Nevil – nogood nogood nogood.*

'Hmm, yeah, yeah,' he answers, his eyes glued to the page, his fingers tracin a line up and down the paper.

'Well ... Jean ... I'm off to bingo, now.' *Geez, seems like a woman's been tryin to get over there all bloody day.* 'Jean, love—' *That'll scrap him.* 'If anyone knocks on the door promise me ya won't answer it, okay?'

'Why, Mum? Is it the way I look?' He brings his head up, chewin on his bottom lip.

'Love, ya know what they're all like. I don't want em here tryin to bash ya. They'll kill ya, love. Ain't nothin Uncle Booty can do bout that.' I sigh, wonderin if it's safe to leave the house at all. Dreadin the possibility of Big Boy and his mate returnin.

'No, you go, Mum. I promise, cross my heart hope to die, that I won't, okay.' He smiles true like. I decide to believe him. Nevie never makes promises he don't keep. *He don't tell lies.*

'Righto, Jeanie.' I turn towards the door. 'Oh, n none a that bloody singin, right?'

'Right.' He reaches into the beer carton and pulls a long one out.

★

'Legs eleven, forty-four out the door, twenty-eight don't be late, fifty-two a red shoe.'

'Bingo!' I hold up me card and jump to me feet, me heart thumpin with excitement.

'Missus Dooley takes the jackpot!' Hettie Bennet yells, as she reaches for me card. I offer a weak grin to all the losers. *Yeah, finally a woman's won somethin. After all this time n now I win.*

Dotty Reedman gives me a sour-as-curdled-milk look while she tears up her card then flings the pieces across the hall.

'Cheat,' she mutters, glarin at me whit small, you-total-bitch eyes.

Pretendin not to hear her, I tap Hettie on the shoulder. 'Any tea n biscuits today?'

'Oh yes! Come on in the tearoom.' She laughs and offers her hand to pull me up out of me seat. 'Good win, Mave. The jackpot's gone up to five hundred dollars today!'

'Mavis, Mavis.'

I turn towards the voice. 'Hello Dotty.' I flinch from her spiteful green gaze.

'Where's Nevil? Keeping out of trouble, is he?' She offers a smartarse smile.

'He's sick. Anyway, what trouble ya mean?' Me hands start itchin, I curl me fingers into em.

'The usual. Smoking drugs, drinking, and annoying some of the better people in this town.' She smirks, her eyes doin me from head to toe.

'Nev's not like that, *Dotty*! He's one a the good fellas.

Spose you heard that from the gossip, did ya?' I tap me foot on the wooden floor, each tap buildin as I watch her sharp eyes. *Taaappp. Tapppppp. Dotty an ugly bat.*

'I don't gossip, Mavis Dooley. I saw him last week down at the hotel drunk as hell. Yep, swearing and acting up a real riot.' She curls her lip back, runs her eye over me faded ol dress, then shrugs.

'And the others in this town don't do that?' I rip in, feelin Hettie's grip tighten round me shoulder.

'Not as bad as *your* son. You should keep a leash on that *menace*!' As she barks her face turns blood-red.

'You ... you bitch!' I scream. 'My son's not the only one!'

'He's *a queer bird* that Nevil. Always thought he was a six pack short of a carton. Few things up here missing.' She points to her horse head, a wide smile runnin cross her face.

'Fuck ya! Ya cow, ya dirty white bitch!' I yell, bustin a seam, and lunge at her.

'Missus Dooley! Missus Reedman! Ladies, stop! Oh my God!'

Me hand smacks Dotty hard cross the head. Her big high hair collapses as she reels back in her chair. Her face colours up bright red n her gob drops open as she glares up at me – green eyes full a spitty fire. *Sayin em rotten things bout me boy. Who she is!*

'Oh God! Ladies, now that's enough!'

Suddenly I feel an arm round me shoulders, a pair a strong hands grips me tightly.

'You right?'

I turn round and see Terry Thompson, the groundsman for the bingo hall.

'Um, yeah.' I watch as one of Dotty's big-notin mates wraps an arm round her.

'Mavis, you okay?' Hettie asks, leading me to the tearoom.

'What's wrong whit her? Gee, she's a real cow that one.'

'A bad loser. Don't worry bout her, Mavis. She's the biggest stickybeak in the whole town *as we all know*.' Hettie laughs as she sits me down.

'Thanks, Terry.' I smile at him, smoothin down the front of me crumpled dress cross me chest.

'It's right, Mave.' He offers me a cheeky grin.

'You watch her, Mavis. She's bound to get a bee in her bonnet over this. Damned spiteful woman that she is. It was only last week she had Joseph and me divorced. A regular gossip carrier.' Hettie's eyebrows shoot off her face as she puts the tea in front of me.

'The likes a her don't worry me, Hettie. I'm used to the way this town talks bout everybody. Why, last month they had Terry here packin up n movin to Asia!' I look at Terry and gut into laughter.

'Asia. A man must be rollin in dough, eh?' He laughs, reaching for his tea cup.

'How is Nevil?' Hettie looks up at me, floatin a shortbread biscuit in her tea.

'Nev? Well, he's okay. He's gone to ... um, he's gone to Tafe. Yeah, he's studyin at the Tafe in Bullya. Ain't much here for em is there?' I almost bite me tongue, knowin whit shame yet another lie is passin me lips. *A woman gotta try to keep on one story. Things are gettin too dicey. Bound to get caught out, fer sure. Yep, any day now.*

'Well, good for him. Yes, I've always said to Joseph, there's a lad will do well for himself. Always thought young Nevil was a deep type. Can really see it in that sombre face of his. A what d'you call it … an introvert. Reminds me very much of my own boy, Travis. Mark my words, Mavis, you've got a fine son.' Hettie rinses out her cup. I grin whit guilt behind her back, her words echoing in me mind: *fine son, fine son.*

I look across at Terry and find him starin at me in a funny sorta way. Somethin on me face?

'Caught a yellowbelly yesterday. You eat it?' Terry pulls up a chair next to me. *Close like.*

'Fish, yeah, love em.' I smile; the truth comes to me that Terry's offerin more than fish. *Ooowwhhh, could it be that love is in the air? Aaarrhhh, wake up to yeself, woman. Not a teenager any more.*

'I can bring it over for you if you like. Nice size.'

'Bring it over. No, arh, I can come to your place.' I almost lose it and tell yet another lie. *Geez, watcha mouth there, ol girl. Ya wadin in nough shit to fill a dry river bed.*

'Mavis, I'm off, love. See you Wednesday?' Hettie casts a knowin look towards Terry then back at me.

'Yeah, Wednesday,' I answer, watchin as she goes out the door. I turn to Terry.

'Tonight?' he asks, hope lightin up his eyes.

29

'No Terry, today.' I stand up, brushin back me hair. *Now what would Terry, handsome good lookin Terry, see in somebody like me?*

'That's a pretty frock. You look good in it, Mave,' he says, gettin to his feet.

'Ya reckon?' I smile nervously, me stomach churnin. *Pretty frock, now that a bare-faced lie! Friggin look like a bundle a walkin washin.*

'Good nough to eat,' he laughs, runnin his fingers through his thick black hair.

'Yeah, ya a real ol Casanova, Terry Thompson,' I throw over me shoulder as I walk outta the room, wigglin me big butt as I go. *Get a load a this!*

'This arvie, then?' he calls out.

'Jus like I said,' I answer smooth like. *Don't want the man thinkin a woman desperate or somethin. Like he the only one I can get. Which he is, eh.*

I walk outside into the bright day, tryin to decide what to do whit five hundred dollars. As I go past the car park I see a mob of women gathered round Dotty Reedman, whisperin and laughin.

'Black bitch.' I hear one of em mutter as I go by.

'White bitches,' I answer, then bare me gnashers at em. *Jealous dogs.*

As I go into town I think about everything that's happened in the day and wonder if tamarra things'll get better. Mebbe tamarra Nev'll wake up to hisself. Mebbe I'll squander all me bingo money, on what I dunno. An mebbe Terry'll change his mind bout me, realise I'm too old, ugly, whatever. Will Booty call n check Nev out? Will Dotty spread any rumours bout me? *Probly.*

'You got a visitor?' Terry asks, plonkin the fish on his kitchen table.

'No, why?'

'Thought I seen a woman hangin washin on the line. I drove past that way today.' He cuts the head off the fish.

'A woman? Nah, ya seein things, Terry.' I swallow the lump in me throat, hopin me guilty face don't give me away. *It were Nevie he seen. I feel it in me gut.*

'It was a woman, Mavis. She had on a pink dress and curlers on her head.' He looks at me, fish guts danglin from his hand.

'Don't be mad, Terry Thompson. Ya been on the piss again, eh?' I squirm on the chair.

'Don't touch it much any more. But yeah, it were a woman I saw. Matter of fact a man nearly stopped to say gidday to her. Thought she might a been one a your mob from out of town.' He wraps the fish in newspaper.

'No. Ain't none a me mob come near me much. Could a been ol Missus Warby ya seen. She's mad as a cut snake that ol lady. Caught her in the laundry one day tryin to flog the Omo!' I laugh. *Easy now.*

'Weren't Missus Warby. This one was young. Good-lookin too!' He grins, and sits down beside me.

'Nah, ain't no one there at me joint. Less it were Gracie doin some washin.' I feel him close in on me.

31

'Gracie don't have shoulders like that. Come on, Mavis, what's the secret?'

'Secret? Ain't no secret. Could a been anybody for all I know.' I shrug me shoulders, tap the table whit me fingers. *Plenty secrets.*

'Nope, don't think so. You tryin to keep her away from me, eh? Come on, Mave, I ain't gonna bite her head off now, am I? I'm a gentleman, that's me, a real gentleman.' He places the wrapped fish in front a me then gives a cheeky smile.

'Terry, if I had somebody there I'd tell ya. Maybe it were that friend a Booty's. He sees a woman that lives over the other side a the railway line. Ain't met her yet, but I told Booty she was welcome at my place anytime.' I wish I coulda thought up somethin else. *Wish I could a told a better lie.*

'That's who it would a been then. Well, honeybunch, I gotta go to the Bowling Club and cut some lawns. Wanna lift home?' He stands and grabs the car keys off the table.

'I'll be right. Walkin never killed nobody.' I pick up the fish and go out the door.

'Hey, Mavis, what you doin tonight?' Terry calls out.

'Goin to bed,' I answer and continue down the street.

I amble homeward deep in thought when suddenly I hear a voice.

'Missus Dooley. Missus Dooley, wait up!' Big Boy gasps as he runs up behind me.

'Hey there. Where ya off to?' I clutch the newspaper dreadin all his questions.

'Hear Nev's pissed off. Just seen Gracie and she told me.' He flexes his arms, watchin me, his face say that he suss.

'Oh, yeah. Um, he went away for a bit.' I stare at the bitumen, silently cursin Gracie and her big trap.

'When's he comin home? Hope he's back for the game. I heard the Rammers got a new bloke and, man, he's sposed to be real good. Still, the Nev'd sort him out for sure.' Big Boy moves from one foot to the other, pumpin his shoulders up n down, starin at the parcel of fish in me hands.

'Don't rightly know. Spose he'll be back when he's ready. His ol Mum can't tell him what to do and when to come home.' *Wish he'd just go way and play whit his football.*

'Okay, Missus Dooley. When he gets back you tell him us mob's waitin for him to get down to the clubhouse, eh?'

'Righto, love.' I watch him through narrowed eyes as he jogs back down to the corner. Suddenly he swings round and comes halfway back to me.

'Who's the sheila at ya place?' He points towards me house.

'A friend,' I reply, quickly turning to make a fast dash home. As I walk up the creaky steps I notice a piece a paper stuck under the doormat. I pull it out and read: *It's no good Mum. Nev's missing and I'm going to look for him. Love from Gracie.*

'Jesus Christ!' I throw the note on the lawn and go into the house slammin the door behind me. Sighin, I collapse on the couch and switch on the TV. Ricki Lake lights up the screen: 'Everyone give a big hand for Velvet Underground,' she says, as a man dressed as a woman walks out on stage.

It never stops.

3

Bitin

'Come on, love. Time to get up.' I open the windows.

Nevil sits up in bed and offers us both a look of confusion. 'Nev? Nevil?' I whisper, lookin into his sleep-filled eyes.

'*Told* you about that. J-E-A-N is the word.' He sighs, then gets to his feet. 'What are you doing, Uncie?' He turns to Booty.

'Get your gear on. We're goin pig shootin.' Booty gives him a glare eye.

'Shit! You know I hate that! Killing things.' Nevil's lip droops. He begins to dress, reaching across the bed and grabbing hold of one of me ol ragged frocks. Booty gapes and runs his bloodshot eyes all over Nevil.

'Uh, uh. No you don't.' He lunges at Nevil and rips the dress from his hands.

'What am I sposed to wear?' Nevil gives me a look that says I should do somethin bout all this.

'Listen to your uncle, love.' I shut me lips purse-like n scan the room for anythin else might be mine.

'Come on, don't fuck about,' Booty snarls, crackin

his knuckles like he's gearin up for some big time rumble.

'Pig shooting my arse! Gee, what are you trying to prove?' Nevil shoots the question to both of us. I look out the window. *The boy gotta be learnin, the sooner the better.*

'Make a man outta ya. That's the problem – you been livin whit your mother here and not havin no man round. Made you a pussy, Nevil. Why you wanna go round bein a pussy, son?' Booty growls, his voice laced with threat.

'Don't talk like that! I hate it when people use such vulgarisms,' Nevil lets rip, then stoops over n pulls his jeans up round his hips.

'What the fuck is that talk, eh? City talk? Ya too good for us now, son?' Booty's face is the colour of coal ash.

'No, Uncie, I'm not thinking that at all.' Nevil stares at his shoes n fidgets whit his hands.

'Right then. Move your arse out into the car. Mave, we won't be back for a little while. Righto.' Booty marches Nevil out the front door.

'Boot, Booty listen.' I stop n wait til Nevil's out of ear-range. 'What if somebody sees him? I mean, I been tellin everybody he's away.'

'Don't worry bout that. I'll take the back street outta town where no one'll see us.' Booty runs a big hand cross his sweaty forehead.

'Oh, right.' I throw a eyeful towards the door, just in case he's listenin. 'D'ya think he's better?'

'Dunno, Mave. He actin like he some sorta poshy

36

white fella. Man'll have to knock that outta him.' Booty shakes his head whit a look a disgust.

'Jus don't be too hard on him, Brother.'

'Nope, but by the time I'm done whit him he'll be back to bein Nevil when we get home.' Booty walks out the door. I stand n watch as they get into the ute, the pig dogs barkin n growlin. Like they suss it might not be Nevie. *Dogs know stuff like that.*

'Bye, love. See you this arvie.' I wave as the car pulls out and speeds down the street. Just as I'm bout to go back inside I see Missus Warby peekin over her fence, her glasses restin on top a the rail.

'Hello, Missus Warby.' I unhinge me jaw. *She's a real ol stickybeak, that one.*

'Hello, Mavis. Was that Nevil?' she asks in a thin, high ol woman voice.

'Yeah. Went out with his uncle for the day.' I grin polite like. *Spose she'll have me standin here all bloody day.*

'Could've sworn I saw him yesterday in a dress. Hanging out the washing, actually. Face paint and all,' she says, her eyes cold n glittery as she takes me in whit em.

'Nevil in a dress!' I let me face go into shock, then not bein able to stop meself I cut it loose, laughin loud. I only hope she don't see the actin job I'm puttin on.

'That's right. Nevil in a frock.' She shakes her head like yes, yes, were that I seed whitout a question.

'No, Missus Warby, Nevil wouldn't do that. A dress, gee, now I heard it all!' I wave me hands in the air. *See a woman stunned.*

'Yes, well, Mavis, that's the very sight that greeted me yesterday when I came out to prune the rose bush. He looked right at me. Fancy! In all my years on this earth I have never, never, seen a man getting about in women's clothes. Not right, is it?' She puckers her lips, looks at me sideways then scratches her head. *The woman seem like she tryin to work out a puzzle. Ain't no puzzle, jus Nev bein a sheila is all.*

'No, that wasn't me Nev. See, Booty's woman, she come over n does her washin here. Musta been her that ya seen.' She gives me a God'll-strike-you-dead-for-telling-lies look.

'Do you need to talk, Mavis? I understand that a woman's lot is far worse than any man will ever know. I know some folk take up drinking and gambling to ease their troubles but that just doesn't work, does it?' Then all a sudden she drops down out of sight.

'Missus Warby?' I try to peer over the fence. 'Are ya down there?' *What's happening?*

'Hang on.' She stands back up n this time she's taller. 'Just pulled the old kero tin over to stand on. Comes in handy. Now, where was I? Oh yes, problems, Mavis.' She wrinkles up her forehead, pushes her glasses back on her nose and watches me like a crow eyein off a carcass.

'Missus Warby, I haven't got any problems. Thanks for your offer of help but there's nothin wrong in me house.' I shrug me shoulders, cursin Nevil. Then a thought comes to me and I wonder how many other people might have seen him at the clothesline. *Probably the whole friggin town.*

I groan inside meself and wonder what Missus Warby will tell her mates from the Bowling Club. *Yeah, can just hear it: Nevil Dooley's gone mad in the head. Poor boy, no father, drunken mother that gambles down the bingo hall with all the other sinners.* I crack a lopsided grin, a small laugh forces its way out just as Missus Warby interrupts.

'Something funny, Mavis?' She narrows her pale-blue eyes.

'Oh no, I was just thinkin bout a thing that happened today.'

'Hmmm. Mavis, why don't you go and see Doctor Chin at the clinic?'

'What for!' I ask, me eyes poppin outta me head. *She thinks I'm the one whit problems!*

'People don't usually talk to themselves and laugh at nothing,' she says, with a look that seems to say: there's somethin bout here like a rotten fish I be gettin a whif a.

'Yeah, well, I've got work to do, see ya.' I make out I is cool n all as I cut it back to me front door, but when I hit the kitchen I make a mad dash to the window and look out. She's still standin on the kero tin and for a buckjumpin second she looks straight at me. I wave to her, tryin to stop meself from wantin to laugh out loud right in front a her.

Instead I close the window. *Just nother shitty day.*

I shuffle me feet, unsure how to ask Lizzy bout this woman writer called Jean Rhys. Finally I say, 'Lizzy, ya got any books bout a woman called Jean Rhys?'

Yep, probably no such person ever existed, nah, only in that messed-up head a Nevil's. Dunno why a woman come here in the first place. Yep, I be lookin womba n all. Best get outta here while the goin's good. I go back towards the door. *Yeah, Nevil made up that name. Ain't no such person.*

'Mavis, where are you going? I can help you, listen.' Lizzy smiles as she brings her head up from the computer and looks at me.

'Orh, I just thought—' *How to say this?*

'I'm here to help you, Mavis, this is a public library and anyone's welcome to use it. You shouldn't be ashamed of trying to read books.'

Ooorrrhh, gee, ain't that just somethin, Mavis tryin to read a book. That's how she looks at me.

'It weren't that. I jus don't – well, anyway, can you help me?' I look down at me feet. *Such shames it be, a woman can't rightly read at any sorta rate.*

'Jean Rhys? Well, that's an impressive start. Now, fill this card out and I'll find some books for you.' She pushes the card across the desk then punches the computer keyboard. 'Here we go, *Wide Sargasso Sea*.' And off she goes and takes it down from the shelf, then hands it over to me.

'Who is she? I mean, who is Jean Rhys?' *She really exists!*

'Jean Rhys was an extraordinary author. She had, of course, a life of considerable anguish and torment. But read the book and I'll see if I can find anything about her.'

'Anguish, torment?' I feel me neck shiver up. 'Was she

a man that dressed like a woman by any chance?' I hold the book up in me greasy hands n eyeball the cover.

'Good grief, no! Whatever gave you that crazy notion?' Lizzy laughs, pushing her hair from her face.

'Nothin. I just – well, I have these mad ideas.' I breathe slow n deep, feelin like as though I'm wadin in a pool a shit that seems to be rising up to drown me whit all me lies and cover ups. *Mavis Dooley, drowned in her own shit. The woman lied til the cows came home. Yep.*

'Here, read it and if you want to know anything at all just ask me, okay? Must say I'm pleased to see you in here, Mavis. All the years I've been working here I don't believe I've actually seen you in here once. Now Nevil, well, he's in here on a daily basis. Matter of fact, he was asking about Jean Rhys too. Must have a fan club over at your house!' She laughs, then turns her attention to a customer walkin in through the door.

'Thanks.' I let the word slip out the side a me mouth. Clutchin the book I go outside onto the main street.

Torment and anguish? Maybe Nev's got bigger things wrong whit him than a woman thought. Geez, have to get him to Doctor Chin. Yep, can't have him livin like that. Course, I wonder if he is gay? Funny thing keepin that a secret from me. Ain't like I gonna push him out. All these years n the boy turns out like this, who'd a thought it …

Lettin me thoughts go I pull in at the Four Square, deciding to buy meself a packet a Tim Tams and a bottle a Coke. *Only thing a woman got really.*

'Mavis, how are you?' Betty Beaton slaps a smile on her dial n gives it to me.

'Oh good, Betty. Yaself?' I show me teeth as I go past her down the dusty aisle.

'Going to the match?' she asks, walkin out from behind the counter.

'The match?' I look at her in confusion.

'The footy match. Believe your boy is gonna shake them up. Such a strapping big lad, Nevil. I spoke to George – you know, the new guy that bought Ray McMahon's pub, and he reckons we'll have a good chance of taking this one out.'

'Yeah, I reckon we might.' I scan the cobwebbed shelves. 'Bloody good coach, George. Oh, and I almost forgot. My Rodney's going around to your place later on to have a yarn to Nev about the game. Anyway, how'd Nev go at Bullya?'

'Oh he did alright. Anyway who told ya he was in Bullya?' I bring me head up from the biscuit packets n look at her.

'Heard on the grapevine. What was he studying?'

'Studyin? Well, um, gee, ain't that terrible I can't really remember.' I look at the cover on the book I'm holdin. 'That's it! Literature, that's what he's studyin.' I smile a mile wide. *What's it mean, anyway? What's Literature, eh? What's that when it's at home?*

'Literature? Crikey, he's smarter than I gave him credit for. Isn't that when you study books and stuff?' She gazes at the book in me hand.

42

'Somethin like that,' I reply, pullin down a packet of fly-shit-splattered Tim Tams.

'So it's true, Nev's back?' She turns as another customer ambles towards the counter.

'Um, yeah.'

'Don't forget to tell him Rodney wants to see him, okay?' She idles back to the counter.

'Righto.' I turn and grab a bottle of Coke from the soft drink fridge.

As I head towards the front a the shop I hear Dotty Reedman's big speakin-out-her-nose voice.

'Yeah, that's right, Betty. Mavis and that bloody old bitch Hettie! Cheating they were! I'll tell you this much, that son of hers is a right criminal. Why, it was only last month he belted into my Jerry. Claimed Jerry called him a coon. If he didn't act like an absolute arse Jerry wouldn't have said nothing.'

'Is that right, Dot?'

'Yes, Betty, that's the truth. It's not like Jerry does these things for the fun of it. I always suspected there was something wrong with that Dooley kid. And listen to this! Missus Warby told me she saw Nevil walking around in the backyard *with a woman's dress on!*'

'That's a load of bullshit!' I cry out n let me legs rush forward, me ol heart tremblin. *I can't take it any more. Won't listen to her gossipin bout me boy.*

'Oh yeah?' Dotty cocks her plucked-to-nothin eyebrows at me.

'Missus Warby reckons she saw a horse in the yard last

43

week, so I wouldn't pay any mind to what she says. Only a simple-minded woman would believe Missus Warby n her gossip.' I slam the biscuits n Coke on the counter. *See now, look what ya done. I'm pissed off now.*

'That's the reason you drink, is it?' Dotty throws me a sly smile, like a cat whit a rat in its mouth.

'Jesus Christ! Spose she done tole ya that too. Or maybe you jus made it all up in that poison little head a yours,' I let me voice snake over. *I be spittin venom soon.* Me hands start shakin ready to smack her cross her smug dial.

'Sorry, Mavis, I certainly didn't make *that one* up. The whole town's talking about it, in case you didn't know.' She blinks back at me, then straightens down the hem of a tiny dress.

'Keep way from me, Dotty. Yer the one in this town spreads all the gossip. Spiteful, that's what ya is. As for Nevil bashin Jerry, well, good job!' I split me gob. Hope that hits her hard.

'You – you – you – black gin!' she squeals outta her pinkish face, shakin a weak, freckled fist at me.

'Piss off.' Me eyes fall into slits, burrin up ready to tackle her on to the floor.

'I'll get you, Mavis. Mark my words, I'll get you!' she hollers over her shoulder then stomps outta the shop, like the woman throwin a kid turn.

'Yeah, n I'm so *scared*.' I laugh out loud. Deep down me gut crawls.

Betty shakes her blue-tinted head as she opens the cash register, *ping, ping*. 'I'll tell you this, Mavis – be careful.

Someone as spiteful as Dotty can do plenty of harm in a little town like this.'

'Yeah, that a fact. Most fellas here in Mandamooka know what she's like, eh.' I look at me biscuits. *Only Dotty could mess a woman's day up. All a her fuckin bout.*

'Still, I'd be ready for anything with her. Don't get me wrong, I like Dotty but I know her type.' Betty flicks her eyes at me then hands over the change.

'Well, I gotta live here too. I'll do my best at dodgin her.' I laugh, but don't really find anything funny at all.

'Wouldn't you think she'd come up with something better than a story about Nevil wearing a dress! Biggest load of crock I ever heard!' Betty bursts out, her face shading pink as she laughs.

'Hmm, yeah. Look, Betty, I gotta take off. See ya later.' I head out the door, the bag a Coke, biscuits and the book feelin like they weigh a ton. *Weighin a woman into the ground.*

Doctor Chin drums his fingers on the table and watches me with a frown. Finally he says, 'Marijuana. Long-term use can cause a certain amount of paranoia. Stress can cause a person to react in unpredictable ways. Drinking to excess is another factor. With all these things combined it is possible for Nevil to think that way.' He pauses. 'Lastly, if he is gay then there's nothing you can do. Except maybe talk to him about it. If you're really concerned then bring him in to see me.'

'His father – could it have somethin to do whit his father leavin all those years ago?' I clutch me purse.

'Missus Dooley, I'm not a psychiatrist. I cannot give you an answer to that question. Maybe you should speak to Nevil about it. Perhaps he does miss his father.' Doctor Chin nods n rubs the side a his face like he's deep in thought.

'I jus dunno any more. Jus dunno what Nevil's up to.'

'Mavis, don't you worry too much, okay? I should check your blood pressure while you're here,' he offers, fiddlin whit that doctor thing round his scrawny neck.

'Not today, Doctor. I'll see if I can bring Nevil in tamarra.' I walk back into the waitin room wonderin if all a those things the doctor sayed done gone to Nev's head. I begin to go out the door when someone calls, 'Where ya goin, ol girl?'

I turn round. It's Gwenny Hinch. 'Hey there. Whatcha doin here at all?'

'Oh, not much. Jus a bit a stress.' She looks away from me, her mouth twisted to one side.

'Yeah, Big Boy playin up, is he?' I watch the way her eyelashes flutter and the way her hand shakes.

'Nah, it's jus stuff that's all.' She bites the corner of her mouth.

'Yeah, well, ya wanna talk bout it?' I drop me arse down beside her.

'Nah, not really. It's jus that … oh, never mind.'

'Man problem?' I squint me peepers at her.

'Somethin like that,' she mumbles.

'Well, love, who ya seein now?' I sly on at the way her eyes shift all bout the room.

'No one much. Oh look, Mave, I jus don't wanna be talkin bout it today. Hey, Nevil in the match or what? Heard Dotty the other day at the pub there sayin stuff bout him. Trust Dot, hey.'

'Dotty! What that thing be *sayin now*!' I gawk into her face, red rage buildin as I pictcha Dotty runnin Nev down to the lowest.

'Jus that Jerry gonna whop Nevil's black arse n that if you're thinkin ya can do anythin bout it then yer flat out wrong. Oh yeah, n that Nev got a dirty secret.' She half-smiles.

'The bitch!'

'Everybody knows she's a wanka, Mave. Don't worry bout the white bitch.' Gwen takes a hunk a fingernail into her gob.

'She's trouble. Don't ya listen to that one, Gwenny. Lies is all she's good for. Hates me cos I took the jackpot out at bingo. That woman got a real mean streak bout her, childish like.' Me gut rock-n-rolls whit rage.

'Reckoned she was gonna do ya over one a these days. Yep, she hate ya guts, ol girl. Be watchin my step if I was you.' She points to me feet.

'Jesus! She never gives up! Well, I've gotta be off, love. If you wanna come round some time, ya welcome, okay. Jus not this week. Ya don't have to be shy whit me, Gwenny. If a woman can help ya out I will n ya know it.' I leave her whit a smile and step outside into the

47

oven-hot day. *I wonder what's bitin Gwenny? What's bitin the Reedman bitch?* Whit these thoughts, I cut it down the hot bitumen.

4

Sandalboy

The white hatchback crawls down the street, slowin every now and then, the skinny-thin wheels crunchin the gravel as it creeps along. Straight out like I knowed this car don't belong in this town, *too good lookin*. I sit down on the steps, tea in hand, Tim Tams beside me, and watch as the driver revs the motor and swings the car round to drive down my side a the street. I shade me eyes gainst the sun and watch as it pulls up near the front gate.

A tall, blonde-haired man gets out. Leanin one arm on the car door he calls out, 'I'm after Nev Dooley, does he live around here anywhere?'

'Yeah, here.' I get to me feet. Curiosity drives me towards the gate.

'Oh, you're his mum?' he asks in a soft voice.

'Reckon so, n who're you?' I read the black print on his neatly ironed, spotless t-shirt: *Foxy Loxy*.

'A friend.' He smiles, reachin into his jeans pocket and bringin out a packet of menthol cigarettes.

'A friend, that's ya name?' I eye off his girlie face.

'No, sorry. I'm Trevor Wren Davidson.' He laughs sorta nervous like, then lights up his cigarette.

'Oh, where ya from then?' I look down at his sandal-dad feet. This fella is definitely in wrong territory round here, the sandals done tole me that.

'The city. Thought I'd come out west and see how Nev's getting on.' He drags on his smoke.

'Yeah, he's good, out pig shootin whit his Uncle Booty. Dunno when they sposed to be back.' I shrug me shoulders. *Funny sorta turnout this one.*

'Oh damn! I really wanted to see him. It's rather important.' His shoulders hunch down as if it were the worst news in the world, Nevil not bein at home.

'Had a long drive, eh?' I watch his face, feelin a little bit sorry for him.

'Yes, Missus Dooley, you could say that.' He flicks the cigarette butt across the road.

'Well, love, wanna come in for a cuppa?' I flash me pearlies at him.

'That'd be fabulous.' He follows me into the house.

'Pull up a chair.'

'Thanks. And how has Nevil been?' he asks, his eyes slidin round the messy room.

Knewed a woman shoulda cleaned it up. Shame peoples gawkin at me filthy kitchen. But orrhh, woman's been busy, that's a fact.

'Pretty good. How'd you know Nev?' Me suss creepers run up me spine when I notice the way he flicks his hands about. *Funny moves.*

'Well, I – I met him at the – oh shoot! I can't think, but I believe it was when I came out this way last year.' I seed the way his eyes trackin the room. *Like he don't wanna look at me.*

Knowin that he's pullin a fast one on me I push on. 'Last year? How come ya didn't come round then?' I place the tea in front a him. He got them big brown cow eyes. But they ain't stupid. A woman can see that all right.

'Didn't think it was good manners.' He takes a sip of tea.

'Gotta girlfriend?' I burst out.

'Oh, well, yes.' He frowns at me as though like he's lookin at a lunatic.

'Sssooo, you like Jean Rhys?' I play me ace. *Gottim, gottim. Bingo!*

'Jean Rhys? Yeah, sure – um, Missus Dooley, are you feeling well? I mean, you look slightly ill.' He peers at me.

'Yeah, I'm well. The question is, are you?' I feel an oily grin crack me face.

'Why, yes,' he answers, his eyes on the door like it offers a fast escape.

'You city fellas have funny ways, doncha? Real *queer* sorta ways.' I purse me lips, determined to put an end to all this before Nevil comes back. *A wile card. He be that.*

'Sorry, don't know what you mean.' He wrinkles his forehead and pushes his teacup cross the table.

'I think ya do. Why ya wearin *women's sandals*!' I have him! Fer sure there's only one one answer to that. The right answer in me book. *Mavis Dooley ain't no fool.*

'Missus Dooley, is there a problem?' His eyes dart round the room.

'Ain't never seen no man gettin bout in *sandals*. Why you wearin em for, eh?' He looks like a rabbit caught in headlights. *Like I gonna skin him up like.*

'You can have them if you like. I mean, I only wear them because my feet sweat in shoes.' He stands up lookin ready to run out the door as fast as his skinny legs'll carry him.

'Do ya love Nevil?' Me nostrils flare, sweat breaks out on me forehead n me teeth ache. *He better!*

'Sure. He's my best mate,' Trevor answers, standin up n takin a small step backwards.

'He's gotta *girlfriend*, ya know. Gracie. Beautiful. She loves Nevil. I want her to be me daughter-in-law. Do you know bout that? Cos I ain't the type a woman ya mess whit, right?' I snarl, wonderin if he's the one done started all this Jean Rhys crap. *Cos he look womanish. Yep, his deli-cate liddle hands tell me that.*

'Yes, Missus Dooley. Look, I've got to go. Can you please tell Nev I'll be down at the Two Dogs,' he says, inchin long the kitchen wall.

'Might.' I throw me hands on me hips.

'Bye, Missus Dooley.' He gives a tiny smile, then hurries out the door.

I jump to me feet and race to the window, watchin as he turns and stares back at the house with somethin like fear on his face.

'Queero,' I whisper, noticin he walks the same way

as Nevil. Silently I curse meself for being so straight out when I shoulda conned him long. Shoulda asked him a lot a questions. *Yep, shoulda kept him here.*

I turn me head when I hear the sound of a car tearin up the road, comin round the corner full-bore. Booty's ute speedin long down the street, black smoke spewin from the tailpipe, the motor soundin like it gonna give up the ghost any minute, n the dogs in the back barking wild. Suddenly Booty brakes so hard the pig carcass on the back flies off the hooks and lands at Trevor's sandal-wearing feet.

Trevor stumbles backward, falls on his arse, and screams woman-like when the bloodied pig head – dead eye hangin outta one side a the skull, ears torn, big mouth barin its dirty long gnashers – lands smack in his lap. Hollerin like a madwoman he's tryin to get to his feet when the dogs come tearin cross the yard towards him.

'Back! Get back, ya fuckas!' yells Booty, his face grey as he jumps from the car and runs after the dogs. 'Deadman down! Deadman down!' Sweat is pissin down his face, spit flyin from his gob, arms flappin wild in the air as he gallops over to the blabberin bawlbaby.

Knowin Booty's command, the dogs back off, tails between they legs. They whimper over to the ute and slide underneath.

Nevil races forward, his face clouded over whit a look a horror n like he can't believe his eyes. 'You right, mate?' he asks, reachin down to haul Trevor to his wobbly feet.

'I – I – I think so,' Trevor heaves, blood and pig gut clingin to his jeans.

Poor scared crapper. 'Bring him inside,' I yell, feelin a ripple of sorry for him. *The boy looks goonary. Probly shit hisself n all.*

Nevil puts an arm around Trevor and walks him into the kitchen. 'Get him a towel, Mum,' he says, leading Trevor to a chair.

'Fucken mutts. That's the problem with em, chase anythin. Get that smell a blood an they off like fucken rockets.' Booty sounds cross but there's a lotta pride in his voice. 'Best fucken pig dogs this side a the black stump,' he adds.

'Ya right, love?' I look at the shakin, white-faced Trevor. *He definitely not right.*

'Well, Mum, he's just nearly had his bloody guts ripped out.' Nevil shakes his head whit a look of disgust and scowls at Booty.

'They would'na hurt a fly. Don't be a pussy, son,' Booty booms, grinnin from ear to ear.

'Nevil, take your friend and show him where the bathroom is. He'll need to wash all that off him.'

Nevil mutters angrily and motions for Trevor to follow him.

'How'd it all go?' I turn to Booty.

'Yeah, all right. Anyway, who's that fella at all?' He nods towards the door.

'Nevil's city friend. Ya know, *friend*.' I walk to the fridge and haul out a bottle a Coke.

'Poofter mate, hey? Man oughta get to him too. He got that wussy look bout him.' Booty reaches for the Coke and pours hisself a glass.

'See the sandals?'

'Nuh! He's wearin *fucken sandals*?' Booty scratches his head, knowin, as I do, the boy's got some serious problem. Specially out in this town. 'Be fucked,' he grumbles, lookin at the door.

'Poor bugger. Those dogs scared the shit outta him.' I laugh, then wipe the sweat from me forehead.

'Dunno what's gonna happen whit the game, Mave. If Nevil don't pull his head in then the Blackouts'll be fucked right up. Jeez, that'd be a real shame, eh?'

'Reckon so. Ain't no one plays like Nev.' I let out a big breath then shove a Tim Tam into me gob. *Ahhh, ain't nuthin like a Tim Tam to clear ya scone.*

'Thinkin bout teaching him to box. What ya reckon?' Booty pats his big gut.

'Geez, Booty, boxin?' I scowl at him. 'I ain't sure if that'd be the right thing to do whit Nev.'

'Yep, a man thing. No pussy ever took to boxin. Might get his girlfriend in on the act too.' He laughs, his fat gut shakin like a plate a gelatine.

'Booty, people startin to get a bit suss bout Nev. I'm tellin lies to everybody. Can't keep this up. Then Dotty Reedman tellin the stinkin town, n Missus Warby spottin him in a dress!' I shove another biscuit into me mouth and wonder when all this'll blow up in me face. Knowin in the bottom a me gut that it'll be soon.

'Can't help em stickybeaks, Mave. Only thing is keep a real close eye on him, keep him away from grog and smokin that weed. He'll come outta it. And for God's sake, keep that fucken brainwashin Ricki Lake off the TV.' Booty picks at his teeth with a matchstick.

'I'm thinkin bout takin him to Doctor Chin. Whatcha reckon, hey?'

'Dunno, Sis, thing is I don't think the doctor can fix him.' Booty pushes the chair in. 'Ah, well, a man's gotta get over n see what Brenda's up to. Ain't been over fer a while, she'll have the shits fer sure. If you have any trouble whit em in there, come n get me, eh?'

'Yeah, yeah, I will.'

Nevil sidles in and stands near the fridge. 'Can Trevor stay here? He's sick.'

'Spose so. No funny business in this house or I'll get Booty over, understand?' I point a finger at him. *No homo business is what I wanna say. But I can't be sayin that, not to me own kid. A woman don't wanna mess whit his head any more than it's already messed. No good puttin any more ideas in it.*

'What's that supposed to mean?'

'I think ya know. Might be a nice boy, Nevil, but he sticks out. Fellas in this town'll do him over. It's like they can't stand strangers. Specially men that get round wearin sandals!' I feel so shamed bout it. *What'd drive a grown man to wear friggin sandals out in this country! City ideas. Fucken city fellas n all their fancy ways. Nevil outta his own territory on this one, fer sure.*

'Mum, he's a friend, that's all. If this town wants to

pick on someone cos they're different, well let them. Look at the way they treat us. Yeah, Mum, they treat us like shit cos we're blackjacks! Seems to me like you're just like them now. If it's not one thing it's another,' Nevil says, soundin depressed.

'Why's he here, Nev? Is this something to do whit Jean Rhys?' I hurl the question, soundin unreal to me own ears.

'Oh, Mother! If I could – never mind. One day you'll find out what this is all about. It's just that I need some time out for me. I've lived my life doing what everyone else expects me to do. *And I've had enough!* Sometimes I wish we'd never ended up in this place. But, oh no, had to fuck off on dad real fast, didn't we?'

'Hey, now don't ya blame me for ya father! He's the one that fucked off on us, Nev! He was no good for us, boy. A woman didn't want ya to be growin up like him – drinkin grog n bein a no good bastard.' I watch Nevil closely. *He's nuthin like his ol man. Then again, right now, I sorta wish he were.*

'Mum, I don't blame you for Dad, you know that. But do you ever think about life? I mean do you wish you could of done things you never tried?' Nevil asks, gazin at me whit a serious-type look.

'Well, love, I dunno. Spose I always wanted to find us a nice place n have a decent life. I jus wanted for ya to have a good life, boy. Not like me own shitty fucked life. Everythin I do is for you, son.' I rest me face on me hands n watch him.

'Mum, I mean if you weren't black, poor, whatever, do you think it would of changed anything?'

'Can't answer that, Nev. I always been black n I always been poor. Sometimes I sorta wished I coulda had a proper schoolin like. Ya know, be sorta smart. A woman feels stupid, I spose.'

'Don't talk shit, Mum, you're not stupid. You're smart. Now look here, there's people out there with all their fancy degrees and diplomas, and, let me tell you, when it comes down to it, put them in your situation and they'd fucken freak, cos your life experience is a special education all its own. A lot of people, even smart ones, wouldn't know fuck about life. Yeah, too up themselves to stop and smell the coffee. Too concerned about *appearances*. Yeah, smart people, eh. Don't make me laugh, Ma.' He grins at me.

'Nevil, where ya learnin that sorta talk?'

'Nowhere, Mum, I always talk this way,' he says, reachin for a biscuit.

'That's a bare-faced lie! Gee, sometimes I wonder where ya get this stuff.'

'Ma, I do more than run wild, you know.' He laughs. 'Is that why you're this Jean Rhys?' I watch the way his face muscles move, like I done hit a raw nerve.

'No, not really. There's more to life than this town, is what I'm saying. They can't help the way they are round here. Born and bred in one spot, this is all they know. Shit, none of them been past the friggin Four Square!'

'So, that's why Trevor's here, cos he's not like the others. Is that what ya mean?'

'In a way, I suppose. Look, Mum, I don't really want to talk about this any more.' He yanks the fridge door open.

'Ya know, I'm here if ya wanna talk. Yeah, n I nearly forgot. I gotta book from the library, *Wide Sargasso Sea*.' I lay me cards on the table, watchin as he turns round slowly n stares bug-eyed at me.

'You did?'

'Yep, Jean Rhys.'

'Mum, you don't read books.'

'I do now. Maybe you'll tell poor ol Mum why ya wanna be Jean Rhys. Ya hate yaself, that it? I believe Jean were a sad sorta person too. Or maybe you think yer goin mad, like that woman in the attic? Yeah, love, I done taken a lot a notice a that book.'

'Oh shit! Mad! Hate myself?' He laughs hard then says, 'It's nothing. I can't … forget it, Mum,' he throws over his shoulder as he walks out the door.

'Ya can't be Jean, Nevil. There was only one Jean in this ol world! Ya hear me! Jean's dead as a doornail!' I yell me guts out. 'Ya not *the woman's ghost*! *I'll find out, Nevil Dooley*!'

Sighin I get up, put the cups in the sink and wash them out. As I stand there thinkin I look out the window.

Missus Warby stands on the kero tin starin over at me joint. Hangin from her neck there's some eye spotters. I push the window open wider to get a better view. Then, as I turn my head, I see the copper, Max Brown, stride through the front gate, whistlin as he moves along.

'Oh no,' I groan, then turn back to Missus Warby, who by this time has the eye spotters up to her eyes. *Jeesussuuuschhrrisst! It never rains but it pours! What that copper doin here?*

I hear the knock on the door n I rush out before Nevil has the chance to open it.

'Mavis, how are you?' Max Brown coughs, then runs his eyes behind me, over me shoulder, like I done got somethin to hide. *Which I have like, har, har.*

'Good, Max, and yerself?' I give me best honest-person smile. *See I a good citizen. I'm no law breaker.*

'Oh, in this job things never get better, only worse,' he says, slappin a smile on his face. 'Look, I've received a missing persons complaint and thought I'd better come around and sort this out.' He looks at me, his sunburnt face wrinkled up into a frown.

'Yeah, who's missin?' I chew on me bottom lip. *What the hell now?*

'Nevil. Isn't he?' he asks, openin a notepad.

'Well, he was, but he's back home now.' I shrug me shoulders hopin he don't wanna see Nevil. *That'd knock the piss outta him fer sure.*

'Can I see him?' It's like the man's readin me mind. 'Well, Max, he's definitely here. But he's in the bathtub. Anyway, who made the complaint?' I part me lips into a smile. *Who the fuckery would do somethin like ring the cops! Could it be – nah, even she wouldn't be that cracked.*

'Gracie Marley claims Nevil disappeared and that you don't know where he is.' Max looks at me whit somethin like a flicker of sussin.

'No, no, she got it all wrong. I didn't say that,' I lie. *Gracie gonna be dead meat when I get holda her.*

'Okay, Mavis, I believe you. Tell Gracie to stop wasting my time when you see her.' Max walks back through the gate, but not before Missus Warby spots him.

'Max! Max, over here!' she cries, wavin the eye spotters at him.

'Bloody silly ol bugger,' I whisper under me breath, then slam the door shut. I can't help but wonder what she's gonna say, what gossip she's gonna spread.

At that moment I feel a sickness in me lower gut. Like a premmanishon, what's that word? I realise all this business whit Nevil is like a deck a cards ready to fall. That there probably are no aces in me deck. *That I be doned over like a dinner.*

5

Another Lie

I lay back on the couch and watch as the crowd moves in one long unbroken line down the street, like a black centipede creepin along on its gut.

'Whadda we want – Land Rights! When do we want em? Now!' The mob chants as they push and shove past the police and TV cameras. For an instant the screen flickers and the picture goes snowy like.

'Bloody thing,' I mumble and get up to fiddle whit the knobs.

'Mum, Mum, don't worry, I'll find him.' I swing round at the voice.

'Gracie? Gracie love, is that you?' I peer round the lounge room.

'Yeah, Mum, I'll bring him home, I promise.'

'Gracie, whatcha talkin bout?' I try to locate her voice in the semi-darkness.

'No, he was never one to do things like this … yep, just disappeared … yeah, from Mandamooka.'

'There are grave concerns for his safety?' I swing wildly round at the man's voice.

Suddenly realisation dawns on me. I smack the side a the TV and bend down to look at the screen. Gracie stands in front of the protestors holdin a big sign whit the words: *Have you seen this man?* and a blown-up photo of Nevil holdin a stubbie in one hand and a fish in the other.

'Jeessuuss Christ!' I burst out and scramble full-tear down the hall. 'Nevil, Nevil!' I bang on his door. 'Open up! Yer on TV! Gracie's tellin everyone ya missin.'

He opens the door. 'What?' He looks at me like I'm the one whit head trouble.

'TV, yer on TV! Gracie, she tellin everyone!' I blabber, me hands flyin mad through the air as I point to the lounge room.

'Gracie on TV? What's wrong with you, Mum? Been on the piss, eh?' He grins, comin closer and sniffin round me face.

'Don't talk stupid,' I shout, grabbin him by the arms n pushin him like a shoppin trolley so fast down the hallway that he stumbles n loses his thongs.

'Hurry up!' I shove him forward. 'There, look!' I point to the screen.

'Oh yeah, a march. Land rights,' Nevil says, his voice flat n low as he turns to look at me.

'Get outta the way!' I push him aside and stare at the picture. 'She was there. Holdin a big sign n a photo of ya.' I race over to the TV and switch channels. 'On the news. She was on the bloody news. I tell ya, Nevil, it's true.'

'Port. You been drinking port, Mum?' He shakes his head, disgust paintin his face.

'Talk bout friggin mad. Ain't touched that shit for years.'

'Mum, maybe you should go to Doctor Chin and have a check-up.'

'Why don't ya believe me?' I walk past him and sit down on the couch.

'Mum, I'm not a missing person, am I?' He sits down beside me.

'It were her. I seen her. It were Gracie all right. Standin in front a that mob a land rights fellas. Know that voice anywhere.' *Now why'd a woman go n tell her what I did? Stupid I shoulda told her the truth. Maybe Gracie woulda understood. Stupid. Mavis Dooley, dickhead. Gee, what a friggin crazy thing to do! Now Nev thinks I been drinkin again.*

'Fellas from round here don't go on TV telling lies about people. Is this your way of telling me something, Mum? Is this about Jean Rhys?' Nevil asks, reachin for me hand.

'Bloody dumb question. Orrhh no, don't worry bout it.' I look back at the screen, wishin her to come on again.

'Mum, Nevil's not missing. He's just gone away for some time. He'll be back,' Nevil says, in a sure tone.

'Son, don't talk to me like I be the one whit problems! Was you started all this!' I let me trap loose n jump up to me feet, rage grippin a woman.

'Yeah, how?'

'All this shit talk bout bein a dead woman! Yeah, Nev, Jean Rhys carked it long time ago. Seem she had a lot a trouble too. But that's no reason to be goin round tellin

64

the world that you is her!' I explode, me heart thuddin.

'Don't you dare say those things! Shit, Mum, I thought you understood!' He punches the air with short, sharp little jabs of his finger.

'Ya know what they do to *homos* in jail? Yeah, that's right, Nev, *homosexual*. Gay! They bash em! I'm sure yer little mate in there'd know bout that, eh!' *Take that bit a truth, Nevil.*

'Gay? Gay? You think I'm gay!' he snorts, his mouth droppin open as he looks at me and shakes his head. 'Oh Mum, I'm not gay.'

'That's what they all say. Yeah, Nev, I watch Ricki Lake n know nough that a lot a fellas deny it.'

I walk over to the wall and look up at the photo of Dave. 'Spose it weren't all yer fault, Nev. It were all that bastard's there. Wouldn't make a good father even if he tried. If I coulda got a dad for ya I woulda. Ya gotta know that, Nev. And remember ya like a son to Uncle Booty.' I try hard to hold back the fast comin tears.

'Don't blame Dad, Mum. Don't blame anyone, okay? You're just stressed out is all. One day I promise you'll look back on all this and say, wasn't a woman silly. I'm just going through some stuff now. Just trying hard to do things my way,' he says, and pats me on the shoulder.

'Sorry, love. A woman's a bit stressed out is all, jus too much catchin up to a person. Been so tired lately, must be the blood pressure. Time for me to go to bed, eh.'

★

Nevil stands on top a the bar, singin n dancin. He wears one of me dresses, his face is covered whit make-up. I sit at the back a the crowd and watch whit a chill in me heart as he slides his hips at the men. I glance down at his feet: he's wearin high heels and stockins. His voice rises, shrill and girl-like as he belts outta tune bout bein a woman in love. Trevor struts in, wearin a mini skirt, a cropped t-shirt and a pair a poshy sandals.

'I'm a good daughter-in-law.' He sits down beside me and laughs.

I look at him! 'Are you Mister Jean Rhys?'

'Maybe I am,' he replies.

'I can't let ya take him away. I don't want Nevil to be a homo.' I turn my attention towards the pub door. Big Boy and the Blackouts barge in, throwin a football to each other. Suddenly they all stop and stare with shocked disbelief at the mincin, dancin form of Nevil.

'Dead man down!' they shout n all rush towards the bar.

It's then I realise that Nev, or Jean Rhys as he's known, would be torn from limb to limb.

'Told ya. You bingo thief. He's queer! A fucken poofter!' Dotty Reedman screeches at me.

'Lies, all lies!' I cry out.

'I can't go with a woman who has a fancy boy for a son!' Terry Thompson spits, glaren at me.

Hettie frowns. 'You're a liar, Mavis.'

'He's missin, Mum, and I mean to find him. I love Nevil,' Gracie's voice calls out.

Jean Rhys was one of the finest writers ever to grace the literary world. There will never be another like her. No, there was only *one Jean Rhys,' Lizzy the librarian whispers in me ear.*

'I don't serve Tim Tams to people who don't know fact from fiction,' Betty yells from behind the shop counter.

'A man ain't a man if he can't kill a pig. Nope, he a regular pussy if he can't do that. Got no time for girly boys. They nuthin,' Booty roars, then flings a chair cross the floor.

Dave floats above me. 'He's useless. You gave birth to a faggot. I can't have that, so I'm pissin off.'

'Get him. Get the poofy boy n is girlfriend! Get Mavis! All her fault! Get her get her get her get her get her get her get her get her get her get her gether gether!' they all scream and rush at me.

'No, no, no! It's all Jean's fault!' I scream, me hands punchin into the pillow. Gaspin n outta breath, I wake up. I swing me legs over the edge a the bed n walk over to the window, confused and dazed. The dream was so real that for a fraction of a second I almost believed it all happened. Still feelin punch-drunk, I go into the kitchen n put the kettle on. *Musta been seein Gracie on TV that brought that dream on a woman. Some people reckon dreams have messages. Wonder what mine was.*

I hear footsteps and turn round to see Trevor dryin his hair with a towel as he comes into the room.

'Mornin,' I greet him, wonderin what bed he slept in.

'Hello. Nice morning isn't it. Not like the city with all its noise and pollution. How lucky you are to be living out here in the sticks,' he says, with a nervy-lookin grin.

'Yeah, guess that's true. Now look, Trevor, while yer here I might as well have a good talk to ya.' I pull up a chair and sit beside him.

'Yes, about what, Missus Dooley?' he questions, throwin a quick peek over his shoulder.

'Bout all this shit been goin on. Ya know, fore you came here, Nevil was actin mighty strange. Yeah, thinkin he's a woman n everythin. Now, I can't rightly blame ya fer all this but it's gettin outta control. Thing is, people are startin to talk.' I give him one of my serious, don't-mess-whit-me looks.

'Missus Dooley, I can't tell Nevil not to do those things. What I would like to tell you is that Nevil is a very special person in more ways than one. People like him are sensitive and not a lot of people can understand that.' He wrings his hands and looks down at the floor.

'Special! Special! What's that sposed to mean eh?' *Yep, this Trevor he the one that's ssppeecciiaall. Real special, puttin shit in Nev's head.*

'He's not like the others. Matter of fact, he's not like anyone I know at all.' Trevor brings his head up and watches me.

'Gay? Is that what you mean?' *There, I done sayed it!*

'No, not that … I mean, once in a lifetime someone like Nevil comes along. He's so far removed from all this here,' he says, spreadin the towel out on the back a the chair.

'Movin! He's not movin nowhere! Ya hear!' I shove me face closer to his, tryin to look as menacin like as possible.

'Oh no, I didn't say *move*. I said far removed. Like he doesn't really fit in here.'

'Yeah, mister smarty pants, big timer city boy, where do he fit in? The stinkin city?' I ask, the hairs on me neck standin to attention.

'That I cannot tell you. Missus Dooley, I'm not here to take Nevil away or anything like that. I'm here to help him. Just bear with me, please,' he pleads, big ol cow eyes beggin at me.

'Sometimes I have to wonder if he's goin mad. Loony. If'n he's like that ol bat next door, crazy as a friggin stock-whipped horse. Ain't right, is it? Nev gettin bout in dresses! I gotta live here in case ya didn't know. It be all on my head, this business. People already thinkin a woman's pissed all a the time.' I let a gust a air outta me gob, then get up and root round in the cupboard for a packet of Tim Tams. *Need calmin down I do. No good for the blood pressure.*

'I understand all that. Please be patient a little longer, Missus Dooley. Nev will be back to himself. He's only going through a phase right now. It's nothing to be afraid of.' That's what he says, but his look don't be convincin me.

'He don't wake up to hisself soon then I'm gettin his arse – oops, shouldna say that word in front of you – I'm gettin him to Doctor Chin to check out that head a his. God knows what's runnin bout in there.' I plonk the biscuits on the table and reach over to haul out a bottle a Coke.

'Trevor, whaddya do in the city?' I open the Tim Tams carefully. *Grillin time. He's not gonna be fuckery whit Mavis Dooley.*

'Oh, not much. I – I'm a – well, I paint things,' he mutters, throwin his eyeballs to a poster a the Blackouts footy team tacked to the fridge.

'A painter, fancy! Well least that's somethin I sorta like. Reckon you could do a ol woman like me a pictcha a somethin?' I pour a glass a Coke and range the biscuits on the saucer. *Gotta step real sneak-like.*

'What of?' He clears his throat and watches me hands.

'Two dogs. Nuh, not the Two Dogs pub – Booty's pig dogs. Reckon they'd make a good paintin, eh?' I push the plate a biscuits and the glass a Coke towards him.

'Oh, yes,' he answers, a frown on his face as he stares down at the biscuits n Coke.

'Eat em up. Put hair on ya chest.' I laugh, findin the joke funnier than he does.

'Breakfast?' he questions, eyes wide n his mouth slack.

'Good tucker. I been eatin the same breakfast for – let's see, yep, for bout ten goin on leven years now.' I chew on the biscuit n wonder what poshy fellas like him eat for breakfast.

'I – well, Missus Dooley, I—'

The boy tongue-tied. Probably no one ever done made him breakfast before. Grateful, that's what I like to see.

'Eat up. Yep, cashionally I do stuff like this for peoples, guests in me home. Ain't no one never turned they noses up at tucker served by Mavis Dooley. Matter a fact I be considered somethin of a cook. Yeah, done cooked for a mob a shearers last year. Couldn't get nough a me grub, fancy that, eh.'

I watch him whit chickenhawk eyes as he begins to eat and drink. Knowin ya can tell a lot bout a man the way he eats. I pay extra special tention to him. *What he is? A glutton – or a finicky fella? Yeah, ya get em in all sorts. The way they chew down they tucker, well it say a damned lot bout a man it do. A woman know, that a fact.*

'Very nice,' he says, his mouth smackin.

'Yep, was always the one for makin a good meal.' I nod me head proudly. *He definitely a normal sorta chewer.* 'What people like you eat in the city?' *I gonna track him right down, find out what this honky tonky is all bout.*

'Oh, mostly lentils, organic foods, soya milk and seaweed.' He puts the glass a Coke up to his mouth n gazes at me over the rim.

'Son, you be eatin seaweed! Now I done heard it all!' *Seaweed, what's he, a friggin whale or such? Bet this is the only decent feed the poor crapper's had for years. That's why he gotta eat weed, cos the poor bastard's starvin to near death. Ooorrhh, a woman feelin shamed. Gee, the poor little bastard. Yep, fucken starved. No wonder he gorgin that tucker down.*

'Good food, Missus Dooley,' he says, then pats his stomach.

'Stay here long nough n you'll be walkin outta here like one a them Blackouts, all muscled up.' I push the packet a Tim Tams in front a him. 'Have some more. Put some meat on them scrawny arms a yours.'

'Thanks.' He grins then turns towards the doorway as Nevil walks in.

'Nevil Dooley! Where the fuck!' I jump to me feet.

'Where'd ya get that dress?'

'One of yours,' he answers, shruggin his shoulders, smoothin down the hem, pickin at his fingernails.

'Gee, can't a woman have any clothes whitout ya pinchin em?' I glare at his made-up face: red lips, pink eyeshada n brown red shit smeared cross his cheekbones. *Fuckery. He done looks like a two-dollar prossie. One of em friggin hookers right outta the Big Smoke.*

'Just borrowing it, Mum.' He sits down beside Trevor and gives him a funny sorta look.

I shake a fist at him. 'Don't you dare go outta this house like that!'

'Don't intend to. Me and Trevor have something to do today, hey, Trev,' he says, smilin. Trevor's face has turned green.

'I got bingo today. While I'm gone I be holdin ya sponsible, Trevor. Whatever you do, don't answer the door. Could be one a the Blackouts lookin for Nev. They see you here n they'll have a shot at ya.' I jab a finger in the direction of his feet. 'Specially if they spot those sandals.'

'Don't worry, Missus Dooley, I'll hold down the fort,' Trevor says in a it'll-be-right tone a voice.

'Oh, n Nevil, don't go big notin yaself by doin any bloody washin. That ol piece next door got a pair a eye spotters n she be spyin on us. Right ol pain in the you know what.' I say me piece then leave the room.

As I'm bout to push me bedroom door open, I hear a bangin on the front door I cut it down the hallway. *Now who's this? Max Brown?* I try to peer through the thick

72

glass window but all I can make out is a fuzzy shape.

'I know yer in there. Open up, fer God's sake!' the voice begs.

I open the door n look goggle-eyed at the sight before me.

'Jesus Christ!' I burst out, me hand against the wall, feelin me legs turn piss-weak.

'Mum, Mum, is he home?' Gracie asks through puffed and busted lips.

'He's here, love. What the hell happened to ya! Jesus Christ Almighty, Gracie! Who doned that! Tell me, bub, I'll go n sort the pricks out!' I take her by the shirt collar n haul her inside, not wantin Missus Warby to see this. *Yeah, the ol bat'd probly blame Nev.*

'A fight. Got caught inna fight at Bullya,' she slurs, tryin to see through black-and-purple eyes.

'Gee, girl, how'd ya manage that?' I take her by the arm and lead her into the lounge room.

'Got caught up in a land rights march. Wasn't even there for that. I was tryin to get my message cross the TV bout Nevil bein missin. Orh, Mum, I tried, I really did. But the coppers come n start floggin everyone. Little kids n all. I'm never goin back there again.' She pushes her long black hair away from her eyes.

'Just weren't yer day, love. But hey, Nev's home n he got a friend whit him,' I say, choosin me words real careful.

'A friend? A girlfriend?' Her eyes light up whit sussin.

'Nah, some big timer from the city. Now, whatever

ya do, jus be careful what you say. Nevil ain't been hisself lately. N don't say any word whit homo in front a it n anythin like it's a gay day. I don't like em words to be used in me household. Nevil's jus a little different since … well, since ya ain't seen him.' I watch the girl's face, she look real suss n edgy.

'I don't right know if ya ready for all this.' I sigh, watchin the way her eyes shift round the room like lookin for somethin.

'Mum, what's goin down? Ya don't sound *right*. I know somethin is real suss round here. Yeah, to do whit Nevil, ain't it? Well, look, Mum, I won't take it. I won't. No sir, Grace Marley never put up whit any cheatin wankers in her life n she's not bout to start now. Don't frig me bout, Mum. If'n it's a woman tell me. That the least ya could do fer a girl.' Her pulpy lips twist into a snarl, but then she sorta lets go a the aggro n her mouth trembles. 'Oh gee, don't feel too good, Mum. I gotta get home, have a lie-down. But I'll be back!'

'Ain't no woman here, love, I promise ya. Yep, you go n lie down. Come back later. I got bingo now. I'll tell ya all bout it then, I promise, okay?' I grab her by the elbow n take her back out the door. *Too dicey jus yet. The girl a wile card. Could do anythin. Could say anythin, to anyone.*

'You better, Mum. A girl can't take no more a this. Nevil's my man n I tend to keep him.'

'Yeah, Gracie, I know that, lovey. But poor ol Mum here is been goin round the bend too. Problems,

problems.' I jus hope Nevil don't walk out from the kitchen. *The jig'd be up fer sure.*

'I trust you, Mum. I'll come over after bingo then.' She throws me a wave n walks slowly out the gate.

I grab hold a the door handle n go to slam it shut when I spot Missus Warby perched up on her kero tin, her eyes drilled into me house. *Gee, can't the woman even pretend she doin somethin other than gawkin over here all the time. Talk bout gall. The hide a her as thick as elephant skin.*

'You-hoo, Mavis, hello! Did you go to Doctor Chin yet? Get that drinking and gambling problem sorted out?' The eye spotters swing to n fro on her chest.

'Yeah, I got it all *sorted out*,' I answer, then slam the door so hard it nearly falls off its hinges. *Bloody stickybeak! Gee, a woman can't even fart n she'd be there askin bout it! Gotta put a end to her gawkin if it's the last thing I do.*

'Mum, who was that?' Nevil asks as he passes.

'No one. Absolutely no one.' I carry meself back to me room, me shoulders heavy, me bones weary. I think bout Gracie and how close I came to tellin her everythin. Realising it'd be a big mistake to let her in on Nev's secret, I think of another lie.

6

She's a Sore Loser

'Legs eleven. Ten, at it again. Thirty-two, tell me who,' Hettie yells as she looks at me cross the room whit a wide smile.

'Bingo!' someone screams.

I turn in me chair to see who the lucky winner is. I groan inwardly as Dotty Reedman struts by, castin me a smart-alec look as she moves grandly towards Hettie.

'Hello there.' I spin in me seat to the direction of another voice and look up at Terry Thompson.

'Whatcha doin here today? Thought you only worked here a coupla times a week,' I say.

'Had to plant some shrubs. Anyway, did you like the fish I gave you?' he asks, creasin his face into a smile.

'Yeah, real nice. Got any more?'

'Not less you want to come fishing with me down to the old Drayson Road.' He gives me a cheeky grin.

'Yeah, Terry Thompson, I know all bout your fishin trips.' I crack a smile at him n fiddle nervously whit the ring on me finger.

'Hey, thought I seen Nevil with some other bloke

out the back of your yard this morning. Some fella with white hair. Looked like they was dancing or something,' he says.

'Dancin in me backyard? Oh yeah, well spose that's Trevor's idea. He's a dancer from the city. Yeah, real solid dancer n all.' Yet another lie passes me lips. Vaguely I wonder when God, if he exists, will reach down n hit me bout the head whit a fork a lightnin for tellin so many yarns. *Yep, now a woman gotta cover up for Trevor too. Double the lies. There's no way the town can find out bout him.*

'Why, hello there, Mavis.' Dotty greets me with a fake smile as she comes prancin cross the room, her thin eyebrows arched as she looks from me to Terry.

'*Hello*, Dotty,' I reply, watchin the way she wiggles her hips towards Terry.

'Terry, how are you?' she asks, thrustin out her big chest and showin a bare bit a leg.

'Good, Dotty, and yourself?' Terry replies, his eyes swallowin her tits.

'Oh, I'm fine. Not a problem in the world,' she answers, casting me a sly sideways look. 'Got any of those gorgeous yellowbellys left? The ones you gave me were delicious.' The bright blue eyeshada on her lids crinkles up.

'Can get you some more if you like. I see you won something there.' Terry points to the card she's holding.

'Yep, about time too.' She shows him the card, brushing his hand as he reaches for it.

Screwin me eyes into tight slits, I watch her as she flirts with Terry n I watch Terry as he eats up all her bullshit. *Revenge, that's what this is bout. Revenge on me for Nev beltin that sooky son a hers. Revenge on me for takin the jackpot. Yep, she's a sore loser.*

'You know, Ross has gone out of town for the week doing some work.' She gives Terry a smoochy look whit what's sposed to be a sexy smile. *She all horse. Big, square teeth flashin. Mane flickin bout. A woman almost spects her to start whinnyin. Neigh, neigh, neigh …*

'What sort of work's he doing?' Terry asks, still lookin at her tits.

That's right, Terry. Just let me sit here like a friggin dummy n watch as she tries to do the dirty whit ya on the floor. Bastard. Yeah, Thompson, just suck it all up. Like I'm not good nough for ya! Maybe if I got round wearin mini skirts n my tits stickin out a mile, you'd eyeball me, too.

'Mainly mustering and stuff like that out at the Beaumont place. It gets lonely over there by myself. Sure need a man about to keep the yard tidy. So if you're interested …' She pats down her mile-high beehive hair do.

'Sure thing. When?' Terry jams his hands into his trouser pockets n shows her a toothy smile.

'Whenever you like. Jerry's at training this week for the big game against the Rammers – speaking of the game, Mavis, how come Nevil's not at training?' She turns her attention to me.

I glare up at her. 'Busy. He's busy whit other portant things at the moment.'

'I'm sure he is. Anyway, George Spiros thinks Jerry'll make man of the match. Being the best player in Mandamooka he's sure to take it out.' Her voice is smooth as treacle.

'Dunno bout that, Dotty. Nev'll be there, you betcha. If anybody gonna take it out it'll be my Nevil. Everybody in town knows me Nev's the best player.' I throw Terry a back-me-up look. He stands there n looks at each of us in turn as if decidin whose side to take.

'What do you think, Terry?' Dotty sidles up close to him.

'I think both fellas are pretty good players. Hard to say really. I mean, they're both playing for the Blackouts, so we already got the best players on our side. One thing I'll say bout Jerry is that the boy can run, that's for sure.' Terry's eyes flick away from mine.

You shit! You … you … backstabber! Take her side, woncha! Jerry couldn't play whit himself! Run? Run, huh, the boy couldn't catch a fucken cold!

I feel me stomach rumble and me hands start to shake as I watch the both of em look at me, waitin for me reply. 'Good luck to him,' I say, me arms outstretched, face calm.

I figure this change a attitude will put Dotty off, make her realise I'm not gonna take any bait she throws my way – til she says, 'Do hope he's going to wear the team colours and not a frock,' n takes one small step back.

'Well, Dotty, if that's the way your son dresses then that's not my problem. Instead a blamin me Nev why don't you talk to Jerry. He's your son. Don't turn that story onto me, Dotty!' I burst out, blood rushin up to me face. *There, take that!*

'You're a lunatic, Mavis Dooley! Shit, everyone knows Nevil's over there getting around in a dress! You're the one with the problem!' She shakes her head n looks at me like I want her pity.

'A drunk, that's all you are!' I shout into her gloatin face.

'Come on, ladies. That's enough. Can't see what good it'll do the boys to have you pair spreading yarns bout em. Imagine if the Rammers got wind a that!' Terry motions for me to sit down and leads an annoyed Dotty to the other side of the room.

When he returns he gives me a strange look and says, 'I can't make out what the hell's wrong with you pair. Like youse just won't give up. No good telling the town shit about both them boys. Sure to ruin everything.'

He sits down beside me. 'Anything I can do?'

'Why'd you do that, take her side?' I ask, swallowin the lump in me throat.

'I didn't take no one's side, Mavis. This has got to stop. I just don't know who's worse, you or her. It ain't rightly got anything to do with me. Whatever's goin with you pair is your business. I don't wanna be brought into it, Mavis.' He puts his hand under his stubbly chin n gazes at me.

'You're a sucker, Terry. I seen the way you connin up to her. Yeah, Terry, you a real big timer, eh.' I stare at the wooden table, a sour taste in me mouth.

'Come on, Mave. Just having a bit a fun is all.' He tries a bright smile on me.

'Didn't look like that to me,' I say, jumpin to me feet n haulin me handbag off the table. I stride outta the hall, hearin low laughter as I pass.

All the way home I rage to meself. Each step I take seems leaden, like me legs are gonna knot up completely. *That Dotty friggin bitch! Gee, fancy him gettin up n runnin over to her like that! Leavin me sittin there like a bag a garbage. To think I really liked Terry. Well, I thought he liked me. But oh no, seems ol Mavis Dooley ain't good nough for him. A woman should a asked him if he thinkin he some white fella now. That Dotty, a woman'll have to pull that big-titted bitch into line. Goin round tellin people bout my Nev! Geez, she got a hide n a half on her!*

Gwen Hinch places the hot, steaming cup of coffee in front of me alongside a plate of Tim Tams.

I look round at the cobwebbed cafe walls n see several oil paintings – all country scenes, I note with disgust. Most of em painted by cocky's wives livin outta town. I wonder why nobody paints anythin else – a dog, a cat, a packet a Tim Tams, anythin part from all those depressin reds, browns n greens. I let the thoughts go as Gwen approaches me whit a cup of coffee in one hand and a fag in the other. 'How you been keeping, Mave?' She puts the coffee down then pulls out a chair.

'Not too bad, Gwen. Yerself?' I scan her face.

'Struggling on, Mave. Always bloody struggling,' she says, reachin over to the other table behind her n grabbin hold of an ashtray. 'I saw young Gracie Marley yesterdee. She come in for a packet of coffin nails. Had a bruiser and a half on her. Somebody sure went to town on her. Her and Nevil had a fight?' Gwen taps the side of her cup with her long fingernails as she gazes at me.

For bout a second I have a think on her question and decide which way I'll answer: lie or truth. Finally I make up me mind. 'Don't rightly know. It definitely weren't Nevil, he no woman basher. He knows better. I catch him bashin women, I likely to bash him back.'

Gwen nods her head and wears a look that says: 'On that one I'll believe you.' I watch the way her eyes flicker round at the cafe. She seems quieter than usual; not her loud, happy, kick-anybody's-arse self. Even her hair looks messed up like she'd not bothered to comb it. She's wearin a white, sweat-stained n beetroot-splattered dress that's tight to her body like gladwrap round a sandwich.

'Gwen, everythin all right?' I quiz.

I pick up a Tim Tam and I'm just bout to bite into it when she says: 'Ahhh, I dunno, Mave. Guess I'm jus sick a workin here is all. Sorta day in, day out. Nuthin changes. Have ya ever had a dream, Mave?' she blurts out, her green eyes fever bright.

'A dream? Well, um, whaddya mean?' I scan her face, wonderin if she's full a turps, if again she's come to work half-charged up.

'Just a dream, like you wish for somethin good to happen. Somethin you always wanted.' She sighs, her lips turned down.

'Oh yeah, I getcha. Well, sometimes I wish I coulda done somethin like gone right through school then got meself some fancy job somewhere. But now, all I dream for is that Nev gets outta this town one day n gets a good job, ya know, somethin decent n then gets a nice wife n I'll have a coupla grankids. That's all I ask for. Ain't worth dreamin when you a ol scrapper like me. Nah, Gwenny, I done walked me dirt track.' I laugh, scrapin the chocolate off the Tim Tam whit me teeth.

'Eh, look out. Mave, ya only ... forty-four?' She taps the cigarette packet n gawks at me like I gone in the head or somethin.

'I feel eighty-three. I dunno, Gwenny, it's like when you had a hard life yer not game nough to wish for too much. Like you know if somethin good happens to ya then ya sorta get ready for the bad stuff that's bound to come next. But yer a good lookin woman, Gwenny. You can do whatever ya like.' I watch the way she picks at her fingernails.

'If ya got money ya can do anythin. Sometimes like I think to meself why'd I ever come to Mandamooka. One-horse town out here in the fucken bush. Nothin here for no one. Town's fulla stickybeaks, old people and horny ol white bastards that wanna fuck ya every chance they get. N some fellas thinkin us black sheilas always ready to open our legs to the first cock we see!' She laughs, but I see the way her face clouds over.

'I reckon ya mean Darryl – Darryl Kane, doncha?' I

pick up another biscuit knowin I'll need all the strength I can get soon as that man's name is mentioned.

'Yeah, guess he's one a them.' She shakes her head whit a look of disgust.

'He spreadin yarns again?' I narrow me eyes.

'Yep, Booty's new woman heard him over at the Two Dogs tellin everbody how good black pussy is. And all the other stuff he's sayin bout me.' She gives me a weak grin.

'Jeesus! Where's that wife a his? What's her name?' I choke down the Tim Tam.

'Samantha. She's too stupid. Anyway, she don't believe what anybody tellin her. I mean, it all happened when she was away. Gee, a person's stupid, Mave. Fancy fallin for all that bullshit stuff he tole me.' She drops her head lookin shamejob face.

'He's like that though, smooth as cream on top a milk. Bet yer you not the only one to be sucked in by him. Gee, fancy goin bout sayin em things boutcha!' I bust a seam, feelin angry n sad for her at the same time.

'I just wish I could get outta this stinkin town. What can a person do, eh? No money n can't work nowhere decent cos all I know is how to work a bloody till. I'm stuck here. Cursed to live here all my life and put up whit this shit goes on behind my back. I tell ya, Mave, I'm fed up whit it all,' she moans, eyeballin at the salt-shaker.

'Come on, Gwenny, don't worry bout it so much. You're a pretty woman n can do better than that piece a shit. We all make mistakes. Ain't your fault if'n the bastard sucked ya in. You wouldn't be the only one he had an affair whit.' I tighten me lips. *Why don't this girl jus tell the dirty bastard off.*

'It's Big Boy I worry bout. He gets wind a all this he'll do Darryl right over. That much I do know. But how can you stop somebody from yarnin behind ya back, eh?' She lights up a fag n shoves it in her mouth.

I shrug me shoulders. 'They been talkin bout me for years. Cos see, there's gonna come a day when good ol Mavis Dooley's gonna pull at the bit. Like whit that big tits Dotty. I'll get back at her! Had years to learn her dirty little tricks.' I pick up the last Tim Tam n shove it in me gob.

'Now that you mention it, it was only the other day I heard Dotty tell someone that Nevil's queer, n when the Blackouts find out the truth they gonna smash his fancy arse. Now, whatcha think the ol bat meant by that?' Gwen gives me a certain look.

'It's all lies, Gwenny. Dotty jus got the shits cos I won the five hundred dollar jackpot. Yep, cos it weren't her takin home the dough. Plus she's pissed off bout Nev floggin into Jerry. It's like a woman done killed her mother or somethin whit the way she carryin on bout me n Nev. Like she jelly of me boy, eh.'

'Bloody womba, ain't she? I mean, gee, there must be somethin bitin at her. Ain't normal, actin like that. Maybe you're right, she's jealous of you n Terry? Who'd fucken know. Anyway, where's the Nev? Haven't seen him for ages. He still on for the game?'

'Sure is. Oh he's been havin some problems whit

hisself. Sorta like when a woman gets her period n don't wanna go out. He'll be ready for the game. But Gwen, I can't see Dotty bein jelly bout me n Terry. He sniffin round her like a mongrel dog on heat. The prick! Hangin off the woman's mini skirt like he some liddle kid chasin his mamma. Oh, well, ain't no skin off my nose,' I say, feelin sorta sick in me guts. *Too many Tim Tams.*

'Don't worry bout it, Mave. The day'll come when Dotty gets her just desserts. Wouldn'ya think Terry'd have a bit a decent bein the woman's married n all. But let me tell ya, Terry do have a lot a time for ya, Mave. It's just he needs a little bit a convincin is all.' She flashes a smile then gets to her feet.

'Yeah, we'll see bout that. Anyway, Gwen, where is Big Boy at?'

She clears the table. 'Gone over to see the Nev.'

'He has?' I jump to me feet, almost knockin me cup onto the floor. 'I'll see ya later. Be down tamarra, okay.'

I rush out the door like me arse is on fire n half-run, half-walk home, hopin n prayin that Nevil's not wearin make-up n a dress. I don't like me chances so when I get to the corner I take full flight n pelt down the street fast as my varicosed legs'll carry me. *Oh God. Oh fuckery!*

Puffin n gaspin for air I stand at me front gate, lookin at the house with dread. *By this time I be reckonin that Big Boy's already pulled Nevil's head off n broken his arms n legs into the bargain. Trevor — well he's dead meat no matter which way ya cut it. One look a those sandals n all hell's bound to happen. Big Boy will suss him right off the mark. Yep,*

Mandamooka ain't a town for any big city, big timin fella. Let lone a fella denies he's gay, when ya only have to take a gawk at him to know what's what. Nevil – well, he just along for the ride. Yep, that's his problem, too easy on listenin to other fellas n they mad ideas. Wonder if Big Boy'll listen to me. Maybe it's already too late.

Strapped n weak from sprintin down the road I push open the gate, feelin ready to spew Tim Tams all over the place. Suddenly a familiar voice stops me in me tracks.

'Drugs. It's drugs, Mavis!' Missus Warby pokes her head over the fence, wavin me towards her, the eye spotters restin on her chest as she balances on the kero tin.

'What?' I walk over to her, me legs creakin. *Mad. She's nutty as a fruitcake. Yep, gettin madder by the minute.*

'It's all been going on behind your back, Mavis. Drug dealers are here, right in your house! All these years in Mandamooka I've never seen what those sort of people look like. Today I have. Yes, that's right, Mavis, they've all pulled the wool over your eyes, I'm sorry to say. Some bloke walked right in there with a black port thing, a briefcase. I know a druggie when I see him. They always carry a briefcase!' She firms her lips and nods.

'Drug dealers! Are you outta your mind!' I can't feel angry whit her. I laugh at the serious, no-nonsense look on her face.

'Mavis, what's so funny about that?' She looks at me whit open sussin as her eyes crawl up n down me figure. I try to form the right words n as I look up at her pink wrinkled face pokin over the fence it reminds me of a dog's puckered arse.

'Mavis Dooley! God help us all! I've never in all my years seen such a display! They've got you into it too! It's the Devil's work, Mavis! Turn your back on them! Say "No" to drugs! On your feet woman!' The ol girl hits her fist on the tin fence and looks down at me with a thundery face.

Suddenly laughter is replaced by surprise as I watch Missus Warby's face crumple up and her eyes bulge as she stares past me.

I turn and see Trevor smilin at both of us.

'Hello there,' he greets the ol girl with a warm smile.

The poor ol sheila can't even close her hangin jaw as she gapes at him.

'Did I interrupt something?' he asks me, walkin over to the fence.

'You're still alive then?' I say, and drop me head to check out his feet, noticin he's wearin a pair a ridin boots whit knee-high socks. Relief rushes through me and at that moment I feel like huggin him and tellin him he's probly jus saved his own arse like. The socks, I note whit a sneaky laugh inside a me, look a bit suss n outta place.

'Yes, I'm alive. What am I, a zombie now?' He gives me a confused sorta look.

'I just thought – oh, never mind.' I cover me mouth whit me hand. *Jeesus.*

'Trevor the zombie,' he says, then walks round the

yard, arms stretched out n legs stiff. 'I'm coming to *get you*,' he speaks in a deep, evil-like voice.

'Come on, Trevor, no foolin.' I turn back to Missus Warby and the fence.

'It's him!' The ol girl hisses, her eyes glued to me face.

'Whatcha mean?' I quiz, favourin Trevor with a yep-she's-womba look.

'Drugs. He's the big boss, I just bet,' she whispers outta the side of her cupped hand.

'He is?' I give her a con look of outrage.

Then Trevor taps me on the shoulder. 'Missus Dooley, I thought I'd just let you know Nev's gone off with Booty for the day. He said something about boxing lessons.' He bends down to pull up his socks.

'Boxin? Bloody hell! Oops, sorry Missus Warby.' I grind me teeth together to stop meself from screamin n swearin.

'I'm off over there now. Catch you later.' Trevor turns n strides cross the yard, his baggy shorts billowin in the breeze. *Shit catchers for sure.*

'That's him! Told you, Mavis! Do you *know* him?' Missus Warby adjusts her glasses and radars in on me like a judge at a court hearing.

'Sure, he's one a Nev's friends from the city.' I shrug me shoulders.

'Mavis, I worry about you there with people like that. Did you see what he was wearing? Baggy shorts! That's where he hides his drugs, I bet!' She slaps the fence. Her voice becomes all loud n crazy like. 'I'm telling you that's where all this killing of innocent people starts. Right there with chaps like him!'

Suddenly her front teeth pop out a her mouth, fly through the air n thump down lightly on me sandshoe.

'Phhse, were thas wha I say.' She goes silent, looks down at me feet whit such a look of horror that I feel sorry for the ol girl.

I bend down n pick up her teeth n hand em back. She shoves em into her mouth n not blinking an eye, she begins again. 'Yes, as I was saying …'

'Look, I've got to go now.' I cut her off just as Gracie steps out from the washin shed holdin a stubbie, a joint jammed in her mouth. I groan deep in me gut. *Today of all days!* Gracie staggers over towards us, her legs weak n wobbly. I curl me face at her dirty clothes n greasy hair. But what really worries me is the t-shirt she's wearin. It's got a ugly, green marijuana leaf pichta on it whit the words: *Smile if you're happy.*

'Hey, Mum. Good ol Mum.' She staggers to me, the beer spillin outta the bottle n all down her.

'Gracie! Whatcha doin, girl?'

She rushes to me. 'I love you! I love Nevil!' She laughs, then throws her arms round me neck.

'Hey. Hey, Missus Warby.' She grins up at the ol woman. 'Wanna toke? Might lighten ya day up a bit, eh?' She shoves the joint under the ol girl's face. I swing round in a panic, knowin that Gracie has just given the ol girl more fuel to torment me whit.

'Gracie, no!' I push her away from the fence. When I

turn back to apologise Missus Warby is gone. 'Geez, girl! Whatsa matter whit ya?' I lead her to the house, me head spinnin from the smell of the joint.

'I want Nevil!' She sobs n coughs at the same time, tryin to keep the smoke jammed behind her teeth. *High as a kite. Makes a woman wonder where they get the shit from. Too much Mary Jane, cocaine n whatever else, fuckery whit all they heads, Nevil included.*

'He ain't here. He's gone over to Booty's.' I lay her onto the couch, and force the stubbie from outta her hand. Then I switch on the TV to drown all her noise. *Yep, never the one to have a quiet drink, not our Gracie, have to go the full-on hog.*

'You gotta tell me. What's wrong with my Nev?' she asks, her face slack, her eyes empty.

'Gracie, how long you been sittin in that ol shed out there?' I think I already know the answer.

'Slept there all night,' she slurs, her bottom lip a ledge.

'Why, Gracie?' I plump up a cushion and shove it under her.

'That woman. Yep, I sawed that woman in the yard. Some flash bitch, make-up all over her face, fancy dress n all. That's her, ain't it, Mum?' She watches me whit watery red, sussin eyes.

Before I can answer I hear somebody yellin for me in the kitchen. *Who the fuck that be?*

'Hang on, Gracie.' I race into the kitchen.

Big Boy Hinch and Grunta the Punter stand near the door lookin real proud.

'Hey, Missus Dool. Check out our colours, man.' Big Boy pokes at the guernsey he's wearin.

'Team colours – neat, eh?' Grunta puffs out his chest.

'Oohh yeah, I reckon. Bloody flash as.' I plaster em whit a smile.

'Nev still here?' Grunta asks, scratchin his fork.

'He gone. What, ya already seen him?' *If they belted him then how come they came back here? Lookin for another rumble. I'm jus the woman to give it to em.*

'Yeah, we seen him this mornin.' Big Boy looks over my shoulder. Gracie stumbles into the room whit a silly smile.

'Hey there, boyos,' she slurs.

'Hey, Gracie,' they answer whit sly smiles on their dials.

'Did you hurt my, Nev, eh, eh?' Gracie rushes for em n as I push her outta the road she knocks Grunta sideways.

'Wha …?' Big Boy croaks, his eyes roamin cross me dial then flickerin back to Gracie. He shrugs his shoulders, a slight frown cross his face.

'I tellin ya Big Boy, Grunty, if anybody hurtin me son then I'm the one'll come after ya! Yeah, that's right, me!' I slam a hand to me chest so hard that I almost knock the wind right outta meself. *Oohhh, fuck, that hurt. Slow down, ol girl. Whhooa up there!*

'Who? Who's hurtin my baby?' Gracie untangles herself from Grunta n gives the boys a spitty evil eye.

'Why, what happened to our bro? Somebody hurt him?' Big Boy flexes his muscles.

'I ... I thought—' I look at their blank faces.

'Somebody hurt Nev?' Grunta bunches up his hands.

'Didn't youse?' I whisper. *That's right, Mavis Dooley, put them big ol feet a yours right in ya own mouth. These fellas don't have a jack arse what ya talkin bout. Go on, BIG MOOUUTTHH. Let the fucken cat outta the sack, why doncha. Tell the friggin world!*

'When? Who? It weren't us. We his mates! Gee, Missus Dool, whatcha think we is?' Big Boy look all disgust n hurt.

'Weeell ...' I shrug me shoulders feelin shamed n hopeless.

'He busted up?' Grunta throws Big Boy a deadly look. 'Musta been afta we left this mornin. Yeah, that measely, muthafucken, pox-faced Jerry Reedman, I bet ya me balls!'

'No, look, I got it all wrong,' I say, feelin drained. I walk to the fridge n pull out a six pack. 'Here, boys. I'm just an ol woman n get things mixed up.' I give em the beer as my way of sayin sorry.

'Hey, Missus Dool! Solid! Now, you tell the Nev if that Jerry come round here startin his shit then come n get me n Grunt here, right,' Big Boy uses his best deep n serious I'm-a-madman-when-I-start type a voice.

'Righto, love,' I answer, collapsin me arse down heavy onto the kitchen chair.

After the boys leave I take Gracie into the lounge room and lay her back on the couch, hopin she'll have a camp.

'Look Ricki Lake's on, love.' I point to the screen.

'Ricki Lake, make Ricki fake,' Gracie snorts, raisin a Fourex to her gob n takin a gulp.

I look down at her. Poor girl. So mucked up n all. It's Nevil doin all a this to her. *Little Gracie, me own daughter like. A woman got a soft spot for her, that a truth.*

'Wanna feed, lovey?' I hitch up her feet onto the couch.

'Yeah, good.' She sighs.

I rush into the kitchen and return. 'Here ya go.' I hand her the plate.

'Flash, Mum.' She grins n looks down at the Tim Tams, Iced Vovos n slice a silverside.

'Yep, was always the one for providin a good meal.' I watch as she chooses a biscuit.

'Say that again,' she says between bites. *Yep, that's the thing bout Gracie, could always preciate a woman's good tucker.*

I walk outta the room, me head thumpin, me legs achin like a woman jus ran from Bourke to Mandamooka n back. But the day ain't over yet. *I'll have to go n check out Nevil, Trevor n Booty. Only God knows what Booty's got em doin now.*

I cut it out the front gate n down to Booty's joint.

7

Make Him a Man

I head down to Booty's backyard shed.

The pig dogs sprawl at the door, scarred heads restin tween big paws. I squint me peepers at the biggest of em. *Is it my magination or is that dog startin to look like his master? Funny thing that, how dogs can look uman. Them big ol eyes sorta drill ya down like. Yep, that dog lookin jus like Booty. Hey, lookandsee, a woman gettin mighty myall in the head.*

A closer look tells me there's a deep gash down the side of its gut. *Poor buggers, chasin pigs ain't healthy work.*

The bitch brings her head up n starts a low growl in the back a her throat. Ignoring her I keep walkin to the shed, blinkin me eyes to adjust to the dark. Me nose picks up the smell a beer, sweat, dust … n somethin else. Somethin thick, somethin that feels like it smotherin a woman, like a hot n heavy hand closin round me throat. Then it hits me – it's fear.

I take in the room whit careful eyes. Booty sits back on the dirt floor holdin a stubbie n bustin his guts at Nevil. Trevor's perched on a empty molasses tin, watchin Booty n Nevil, his eyes flickerin back n forth.

I feel sweat pop out on the back a me neck, the heat in the shed is fierce. I get a load a Nevil, shirtless n pissin sweat as he moves round a sack of potatoes that hang tied from the beams. He cuts it round the sack like a dancer, his eyes peeled on it as he jabs n hits whit all his strength.

'If that were a fella he'd have your guts by now – have ya busted from arsehole to breakfast time!' Booty roars, gettin to his feet n goin over to Nevil. 'Mid-section, son. You gotta bring this fucka to his knees! Otherwise this fucka's gonna bring you to *ya* knees, got it!' Booty pelts forward and hits the bag so hard it swings back, drivin him backwards. 'Ain't no fucka ever got away from this here punch!'

Booty holds his fists in the air, like he's standin in the middle of a big time boxin ring.

I nod me head towards him then wander over to Trevor.

'Hello, Missus Dooley,' he greets me whit what looks like relief.

'Hey there. Now what the hell's goin on here?' I wipe the sweat off me neck.

'Booty's teaching Nevil how to box. He reckons it'll make a man out of him.' He shrugs his shoulders and winces each time Nevil jabs the sack. 'I guess that's the way of life out here in the bush.'

'Yeah, no use bein a girl round these parts. Gotta look after yerself, nobody else will.' I hold in a laugh as I watch the way Booty struts round the shed. His fat gut hangs out over his shorts, his bare feet move along like he can hardly carry his own weight, and his big frame moves across the room like a constipated goanna. *Yeah, that's good ol Boot for ya.* He comes over to us swingin his fists and stops in front a Trevor.

'On ya feet, son!' he barks.

'Oh, gee.' Trevor casts me a look of desperation.

Just as I'm bout to unhinge me trap to tell Booty to leave him be, I hear loud laughter comin from the shed doorway. Big Boy and Grunta saunter in. Big Boy carries a box a piss. Grunta's got a blue heeler on a chain. Big Boy's eyes sweep cross the room n come to rest on Trevor.

Booty nods at Big Boy. 'Here, son, git ya black arse over here n teach this migaloo how to handle hisself.'

'Oh gee listen, Booty, I'm no good at this sort of thing,' Trevor says, wringin his hands n lookin down at his boots.

'Talk shit, son.' Booty hauls him to his feet. 'Get that fucken shirt off, will ya.' He pokes at Trevor's t-shirt.

'Booty, he don't wanna do this. Leave him be.' I shake me head. But it's too late, Booty's on a drunken high, and Big Boy's gettin high on the possibility a smashin somebody's face in.

Nevil turns to look at Trevor but Trevor is lost in this mad moment, most probly can't see or hear anythin. *Fear does that to ya.*

Grunta ties the dog to a post n comes to stand beside me. 'Who he?'

'That's Trevor, a *friend* a mine.' I lay down me cards. *If there be hurtin goin on whit that poor boy then I'm gonna be*

*the one whoppin arse. Ain't like he's a scrubber. Not like this
lot, born whit fists in the air.*

'Geez, them boots n socks for real or what?' Grunta
points at Trevor's knee socks n ridin boots.

'Yep, I told him to wear em like that. Good, eh?' I
curl up me mouth n wait for Grunt's reaction.

'Solid, Missus D.' *He knows the score.*

Booty whispers somethin into Big Boy's ear then
turns and whispers into Trevor's ear. I feel the back a me
neck crawl. I don't like it. Booty can get a bit fist happy
n not know when to give up.

I throw Nevil a sour look. He stands starin, hands
on hips, eyes slitted. He knows what his uncle's doin.
So do I.

Trevor, white-faced, shakin like a mongrel dog jus
swallowed ten-forty, swings round n gives me a please-
help-me look.

'That's enough!' I walk towards them. *A woman seed
nough blood in her lifetime already. This little fella they gonna
kill.*

Booty steps in front a me. 'No one's gettin hurt,
Mave. Just teachin the boy some tricks,' he says, beer
fumes comin outta every pore.

'If anybody hurt Trevor then they fight me – Mavis
Dooley!' I throw a fist in the air, all gammon like cos
that's what it's all bout. A gammon game. Cept it ain't
like that for this mob – Big Boy, Grunta, specially
Booty.

Not willin to put me to the test, Booty pats me on the

shoulder. 'Come on, Sis, how ya think he gonna get on down at the Two Dogs? They'd make mincemeat a him. Alls I'm doin is tryin to teach him a few things. No one gonna get hurt.'

'They better not, Booty. Cos I holdin you sponsible for this.' I poke his chest, then walk over n sit on the molasses tin and watch as Big Boy n Trevor dance round each other. Trevor looks like he some ol clodhopper, his feet movin heavy like on the ground. *He don't stand a chance. These fellas gonna flog him stupid.*

'Stop! Come here, Trev.' I motion him to come close.

He looks puzzled as he scans me face. 'Yeah?'

I look round to make sure no one can hear. 'Now listen. That Big Boy's gonna try n hurt ya. I like Big Boy, but that's not the point. The point is ya couldn't even win a fight whit me, son. But I can't stand back n watch you pulped like a orange. Now take those bloody boots off ya feet n listen to this.' I give him all me hard-earned tricks. Everthin I ever learned to survive. *There's quite a few of em.* After our talk he walks back to Big Boy mebbe whit a small hope. *Booty n his shit talk! Teachin em how to fight. Geez, only Booty!*

Grunta eyeballs me. 'What was that bout?' He bends down n hauls a stubbie outta the box.

'Nuthin for you to worry bout.' I purse me lips n step up on the molasses tin.

'Higher, fuck ya!' Booty runs round circlin the boys. 'What ya, a fucken pussyboy!' he yells at Trevor.

The more I watch him the more I don't like it. He's

singled Trevor out for special treatment. *Booty treatment. That means hurtin in his books.*

'You right, Trevor. Just do as I tole ya.'

'Girl, fucken big city girl!' Booty taunts.

It's all a bad mistake. I shouldn'a let em go on like this. Ain't right. Me n me big trap. Poor ol Trevor. I jump off the tin n run towards the boys. 'Break it up, Booty!' I shout, flappin me arms. 'It's gone too far.'

Big Boy turns to look at me, a killer smile on his face. At that moment Trevor throws a wild punch and, like in a slow motion movie, it lands on the side a Booty's head.

Cccrraaacckkkk! Booty's gob flips open and a deep, high *arghwwoooo* comes out, soundin like a injured bull. His arms fall behind him as his big fat frame wobbles n crashes to the dirt. *Whhhumummpp!* I feel me gut drop, I struggle for air, sweat rivers me face. *Fuckery!*

Big Boy gawks at Trevor, his mouth open wide, his eyes bulgin outta his head like he gonna explode. Grunta rushes forward, stubbie in hand, and stares down at Booty like he can't believe his own eyes.

Nevil, his shirt on now, hurries over to stand beside me and gapes at Trevor then Booty.

Me, well, I'm ready to have a heart attack! Ain't nobody ever put Booty on his arse! Nope, none a the fellas round Mandamooka or anywhere else for that matter would even dream a standin up to Booty's big, hard fists. Cept for this skinny, brown-eyed white boy in front a him. He the first. Ever.

Me insides churn, me hands shake n I feel the piss buildin up in me bladder. Trevor has his hand cross his mouth, as like to stop hisself from screamin whit terror. Yeah, terror. Can see it in the boy's watery eyes.

Booty, not missin a beat, gets to his feet, stunned n half stupid lookin. A trickle of blood runs down the side a his ash-coloured face. He turns round to Trevor.

I realise whatever's gonna happen now is right outta me hands. I close me eyes and see Trevor hanged from the beams, stripped right down to his shorts, and bein pummelled like the punchin bag as Booty goes to town on him.

Then, hearin a sharp gasp, I turn to Nevil who holds onto his chest like it's gonna collapse in on him.

'He didn't mean to.' I hear Nevil almost bawlbabyin to Booty.

'Dead meat fer sure.' I hear Big Boy mutter.

'Bad move, bro.' I hear Grunta say to Trevor.

'Nnnnnooooo!' I scream and rush at Booty, blockin him from Trevor.

'Outta the way, Mavis.' Booty pushes past, over to Trevor.

Yep, can see it all: black fella bashes white fella to death in a dog shed. Mavis Dooley – liar, Tim Tam eater, poofter protector, stood by n watched while the white fella carked it. Yeah, that's what the Bullya News'll be sayin.

Booty's hand drops on Trevor's shoulder. *Yep, even ripped the boy's arm clean outta its socket.* Then Trevor takes a stumbly step back, his face by this time white as Missus

Warby's sheets. *Yeah, the boy's face was ripped off, skin pale as a ghost it were.*

Trevor opens his mouth to speak but all that comes out is a squeak. Loomin over Trevor's fear struck body, Booty, sweat pourin down his face, lets out a low growl. 'Fucken punch n a half on ya, Sonny Jim!' Then he explodes into loud laughter.

The boy lives! I can see it now: white fella bashes Booty Dooley in his own shed. Yep, even knocked him to the ground! To look at he ain't much, but … man, he can whop anyone! Not to be fucked whit! I can hear all the town gossipin at once.

I look at Trevor all beamin n relieved as he takes a stubbie from Grunta's hand. *Proved hisself. That he sure did!*

Booty puts an arm round me. 'Mavis, you sure know how to get a pussy n turn him into a tiger.' He laughs n slaps me on the back.

What can I say? All I done tole Trevor was to run away when Big Boy started to throw punches at him. I never tole him to belt Booty one. Gee, a woman's not that mad n all. I run a hand cross me hot face, dust clogs me mouth n sweat drenches the front of me dress. *A woman gonna call it a day.*

'I'm off, boys.' I move towards the door. Well, at least Nev seems back to normal n Trevor's still kickin, phew. I walk out into the eye-achingly bright day when a voice behind me stops me in my tracks.

'Missus Dooley, thanks, thanks for everything.' Trevor walks towards me with a smile, his face returnin to normal colour.

'Why thank me, son? I ain't done nuthin fer ya. Anyway, how'd ya get that punch on Booty?'

'Oh that was a mistake.'

'Jesus! Well, don't go tellin any a them that,' I reply, suddenly realisin I like the boy. Like his ways. *City boy or not.*

'I'm not that stupid.' He laughs. Then in Booty's voice he booms, 'What d'ya think, I'm a pussy now?'

'I wouldn't make a habit of doin that either.' I continue on out the gate.

8

Rumblin On

Gwen Hinch sits at the end of the bar skullin a beer, mumblin to herself n lookin like a sack a unironed clothes. The woman look pissed off her head.

I scan the bar. Then as me eyes take in the room, I feel me heart quicken when I spot Terry Thompson bent over the pool table.

He looks good. His hair combed back, clean shirt, ironed jeans n for once he's not blind drunk. Should a woman talk to him after the way he scoured me up at the bingo hall? Leavin me sittin like a ton a shit as he conned that bitch Dotty Reedman up. Yeah, wonder if he went to her place. I wouldn't put it past Terry to screw her. Yeah, that'd be Dotty's way a gettin me back for everythin.

I walk past him, really regrettin not puttin a bit a lipstick on. *Geez, knew I shoulda wore that red dress! If a woman coulda peeled it off Nev, that is. Yep, Mavis Dooley, ya done it again!* I turn me face from the table as I go by, hopin he doesn't see me. No such luck.

'Mavis, how are you?' He steps out in front a me.

'Terry, all right. Yerself?' I grin, me legs jellied.

'I'm good. Look, I hope you don't think a man took Dotty's side at the bingo there the other day. I mean, come on, Mave. You two are at each other's throats but for what? You both got sons playing in the big match.' He motions for me to sit.

'I'll stand, thank you. Now, Terry, it were Dotty that started all this. Tellin everybody in sight bout my Nevil! The bitch! As for her boy, Jerry, takin out the man a the match, well that's a load a horse shit! My Nevil's gonna take it out! Yeah, n I notice you right up her alley. Far as I'm concerned you're just like her!' I screw up me face and give him my best look a disgust. *See how pissed a woman is atcha?*

'Hey, that's not true, Mavis. Dotty's – well, *dotty*, ain't she.' He laughs. 'She's all right to have a yarn to but a man's not stupid when it comes to sheilas like her.' He picks up his beer and takes a sip.

'Right. Well, I'll see you round.' I turn n head cross the room towards Gwen.

'Hey, Mavis, you comin over to my place for the barbie tamarra night? Got a couple a cod.'

Knowin this is his way of sayin sorry I reply, 'Yeah, what time?' *A date? Is that his way a gettin to a person? Nah, think shit, woman. Wake up to yerself, for God's sake!*

'Whenever. Bring Booty, Nev n ever who else you like.'

'Righto. I'll see you then.' Feelin a lot better bout meself I stroll over to Gwen.

'Gwenny, whatcha up to?' I pull up a stool and sit

beside her. *How long she been sittin here for? Musta been some time by the go a her dial.*

'Drownin me sorrows, Mave.' She grins, her eyes bloodshot, face slack.

'What now?' I watch the way her eyes sneak round the room.

'Haven't you heard? Yeah, I'm supposed to be fuckin old Creekwater Davidson.' She snorts.

'Creekwater! Geez, can't they come up whit nobody else? Geez, only Mandamooka fellas would say things like that! Anyway, who tole you?' I motion to the barmaid. 'A beer.' *There I done it. Yep, a woman back to drinkin. Nev'd skin me face off if he knew that. Orh, well a woman had a rough week to start whit.*

'One guess.'

'Missus Warby?' I dig into me pocket, pull out a ten dollar bill n shove it cross the bar.

'Nope. Dotty Reedman.'

'Friggin hell, Gwen! How many times a woman gotta tell ya don't listen to nothin that horse-faced, big-titted bitch gotta say! You know what she like, Gwenny.' I cross me arms, peerin into her face.

'Yeah, but she heard it from Darryl Kane. That troublemakin piece a shit.' She drops her head, shame like.

'Fuck em!' I explode. 'That idiot wanna be worryin bout his family stead a runnin round makin trouble for you! Yep, that's the nature a this town, makin yarns, tearin some poor bastard to pieces! If it weren't you, Gwenny, it'd be me they runnin down!' I pick up the beer n skull it in one hit. *I feel sorry for Gwenny. One affair n the town's got her havin it off whit every man and his dog. Like the woman'd screw anythin. As though she desperate.*

'Oh, yeah, n that Terry Thompson fuckin Dotty Reedman. I dunno if that be true or not.' Gwen laughs loud n hard and beer splutters from her mouth as she shakes her head. 'The man'd have to be desperate. And you know what else I heard, eh? You sposed to be keepin Nevie boy locked up over there cos he's wearin your dresses n make-up!'

'Who said that?' I feel me chest tighten. *It's all comin back to me now. Caught out. Yep, the lies doin full circle.*

'Missus Warby was in tellin someone the other day. Reckons she seen Nevil runnin round the backyard dancin, full a make-up, wearin one of ya dresses. She mad that old one.' Gwen looks at me then breaks into a big smile. 'Fucken Mandamooka.'

'Yeah, where they can ruin your life with a rumour.' I motion to the barmaid. 'A Scotch n Coke.'

Gwen stares at me, a frown on her face. 'Mave, you don't drink hard shit. What's goin on?' She blinks her eyes as though seein me for the first time.

'Just like you, Gwenny, I got me problems. Number one, over there playin pool. Number two, horse-face Reedman. An some other stuff.' I sigh wearily.

'Terry Thompson? Why, what's wrong with him, apart from that shit I just said? But, hey, it's only gossip, ya shouldn't really believe it.' She shrugs her shoulders then downs another beer.

'Dunno bout that. Seem to be stuck up Dotty's skirt, don't he? Yeah, was over there cleanin her yard up, eh. You can't tell me nuthin's goin on there whit em.' I stare at the floor. *Well, seems Dotty won this one. Yep, ol black-arse Mavis lost out again.*

'Terry was over there?' Gwen's face looks shocked as she eyes me over the rim of the beer glass.

'He sure was. Oh well, ain't nuthin a woman can do bout that. Ain't like I married to the man. If he be wantin Dotty then he can have her far as I'm concerned. Then I got that ol Missus Warby spyin on me joint n cartin yarns, got problems with Nev, oh I jus dunno any more.' I swallow a lump in me throat.

'Oh, come on, mate, don't let it getcha down. Fuck em all, that's what I say. Yep, they can all go to hell. Anyway, what's up whit Nev?'

'Stuff,' I reply, then down the Scotch like it's a soft drink. For a second it burns me throat. *I'm startin to feel better already! Almost charged up. Heeeyy look out!*

'Like what? Big Boy tole me they was all at Booty's punchin on. What was that about? Someone been into Nevie, eh?'

'Jus Booty tryin to toughen him up a bit. You know what Booty's like.' I motion for another drink. *I'm a loose goose. Good one.*

'Yeah, solid old Booty boy. Mave, if there's somethin goin on whit Nev n you wanna talk about it …'

'Nah, Nev's jus Nev.' I shrug me shoulders. *Yeah, jus Nev. The boy'll be wearin me bloomers fore too long.*

'He's still on for the big game?' Gwen skulls a beer. Eyes redder n the spot on a red-back spider.

'Guess so. Gwen, does – you know, does Big Boy ever think he's – well, he's somebody else?' I scratch me head. *Gotta ask somebody bout this. Woman turnin womba.*

'Wha? Like whatcha mean?' she asks, peerin into her empty glass.

'Like someone else,' I croak, me gut heavin.

'Oh, I getcha. Yeah, he think he's a big time football star.' She laughs. 'Only thing wrong whit that. He ain't no star!'

'Like, is it for real? I mean – he don't ever think he's a woman, do he?' I burst out, the Scotch loosenin my tongue. *Watchit, watchit.*

'A woman! Shit, no!' She gives me a drunken look but I see the sussin in it. 'Mave, you better tell me. I ain't like the others in this shit-hole of a town. I'm a woman can keep a secret.' She pats me on the knee.

'Well,' I begin, but as I'm bout to continue I hear familiar laughter. I turn round on the stool and watch as Dotty struts towards Terry. She's all tarted up. Dirty blonde hair high as an ant hill. Mini skirt so short I can almost see her bloomers pokin out. Face painted up like a crayon picture. Blood-red lips, blue eyeshada, rust-colour cheeks painted round like half-bad apples, n eyelashes so long they look like they gonna sweep the floor. Fat tits sittin out front a her like a beer tray, she one flash piece a meat. *Swishhh, swissshhhh.* She fancied up to kill. Me. *Yeeeeoooowwwww.*

I groan, the Scotch races up to sit in the front a me throat. *A woman jus can't win, no matter which way I cut it.* I glance down at the ol house dress I got on, small holes in the hem, faded, too big for me; jus flat out ugly. *Yeah, real pretty, pretty as a punch in the face. Jus betcha me ol dial looks rugged too. Wide as Dotty's arse, plain, fat whit gooby lips, fuzzy hair like a pot scourer, a boxer's nose, thin black moustache on me top lip n skin like sandpaper. Yep, was never beautiful by any means. A scrubber. Bush pig. Weren't like I was ever gonna be some pretty piece. Naahhh.*

I watch Dotty whit green eyes, the way she sidles up to Terry, her long legs brushin gainst him as she bends over the pool cue.

'Lookit that fucker!' Gwen nudges me in the ribs.

'Yeah, check out the way Terry all over her, eh? What, he think he white now?' I order another drink. Rum n Coke. Too much for a woman to take in. Me guts is boilin over like a pot a bubblin stew.

'Gee, she gonna fuck him on that table?' Gwen laughs, and almost falls off the stool. *She well n truly charged now, ol Gwenny.*

'She just doin that cos she knows I like him.' I feel me bottom lip ledge out.

'Check that Terry out. What, he too good for us now?' Gwen's voice edges.

'Yeah, like us black sheila's ain't good nough for him!' I spit. By this time everythin is startin to look wet n hazy. *Fucken Thompson. Fucken men. Ain't worth pissin on.*

Terry glances towards me and taps the side of his beer glass. 'Drink, love?' he asks, saunterin over.

Drink, love? What, suddenly I'm his love now? What bout your piece a white meat, Terry? Yeah, her husband's back in town n you wanna be foolin whit her.

'Hey Ter. Wanna have a drink whit me n Mave, eh? Or ain't us fellas good nough for ya?'

'Whoa up there, Gwenny! A man didn't come over here to get his arse kicked by you. I just askin, do youse want a drink?' He clears his throat and watches me.

'Arrggh, go n get that dolly bitch a drink, Terry Thompson. Mavis not woman nough for ya. Ain't white nough!' Gwen stumbles to her feet and shoves Terry in the chest. Real hard like.

'Bloody hell, settle down, Gwen! This got nothin to do whit Mavis. Me n Mave are mates, eh, Mave?' Terry gives Gwen a pissed off look.

'Sure. Mates,' I mumble, feelin a boot kick me somewhere in the guts. *Don't know why a woman had to big-note herself n come down here for. Shoulda stayed home whit Nevie n Trevor. Terry wouldn'a look at somethin like me. Nah, just no dice there, ol girl. Terry Thompson don't like women like me. See, a woman gets these mad ideas in her head. Yep, Mavis Dooley, all-time loser. All-time fuck up. Jus another let-down is all. Woman should be used to it by now.*

'Mave, I'll see you later,' Terry says, shruggin his shoulders as he goes back to the laughin, crowin Dotty.

'Fucken cunts. That's all they are, the whole lotta em. Ignore em, Mave. You too good for that bitch, anyway. Geez, Mave, look who just walked in!' Gwen gasps, plonkin herself back on the stool, noddin towards the doorway.

Darryl Kane saunters in, wife hangin off his arm as he looks round at the bar. *Cocky bastard. Lookin for some. fresh meat.*

'Fucken dog,' Gwen hisses between her teeth.

'Pay no mind to em, Gwenny,' I slur, feelin the anger hitchin up in me slow like. I watch the way he slides cross the floor like he owns the place, like he's the best thing since sliced bread. All kitted out like some ol Smokey Joe cowboy. *Yeah, him n Dotty a good pair a dolly birds together.*

He leaves his wife at the bar and saunters towards the young girls that sit watching the jackaroos. I take in his form: silky, slimy, n smooth. *I wonder what he's tole that poor sucker of a wife? Probably that them girls are his friends or some such shit.*

'Lookit that, huh. Nough to make ya vomit.' Gwen swings round on the stool, spit-eyes as she looks him up n down.

'Cool as water.' I narrow me peepers. *The snake. No, the snakes – Terry, Darryl.*

'You know what, Gwenny. We should get him back. Do somethin to him, eh? Reckon I don't like it for that two-bit fuckery to be goin bout spreadin filth bout me best mate n all.'

'How do ya get back on somebody like him?' Gwen slumps her shoulders.

'I dunno. Do somethin to him. He can't go all round

town dirtyin your name up. Like he wants to make your life miserable. Friggin white bastard!' I bang me fist on the bar.

'Arrgghh no, nuthin we can do, Mave. Just let it ride. He ain't worth the trouble.'

'Get up, Gwenny! Now listen, go over there n tell that woman a his what's been goin on. Gorn, Gwenny. I'll come whit ya.' I stand up on grog-fucked legs. 'Come on girl, move.' I grab her by the arm n steer her towards the other end a the bar. *There gonna be rumblin on. Yiiiieee.*

Samantha Kane perches up on the bar stool. I stand behind her and cough loud like. 'Samantha,' I say in my best sober voice.

She turns round with a slight frown, looks at me then Gwen.

'Can I help you?' She looks Gwen up n down. *Wwrreeeooowww! Claws out! Hiss, hisssy.*

'Well, you know Gwen here, doncha?' I put me hands on me wide hips n take a tough stance. *Ready to jump the train.*

'Ah, well. You're Boy's mother? Peter Hinch – Big Boy's mother?' She shrugs her shoulders. Like the woman couldn't give a flyin piss either way.

'That's bout right. Now Gwenny's got somethin to tell ya. Tell her, Gwen.' I shove her forward. *Go on Gwen, tell her the truth.*

But Gwen just stands there lookin stunned n drunk as Booty on a bender. Suddenly I see she looks kinda scared. *Ain't like Gwenny to be frightened. No, siree.*

'Righto, I'll tell ya then. Your husband, that thing over there, has been talkin bout Gwen here all over town. Yep, that's right he's been rootin her when you was gone away. Then he got the hide to run her down to the lowest.' I watch the way her face changes – from not believin, to mad as hell, to not my Darryl.

'That's not true,' she squeaks.

'It true, all right.'

'Darryl doesn't do that with—' She stops, then looks at Gwen with a frown.

'Doesn't do that whit what?' I walk up closer to her.

'With black women!' she bursts out, face redder n the pits a hell.

Gwen throws her hands into the air, glaring at her. 'Ya fucken idiot! What? He doesn't fuck anyone part from you!'

'Troublemakers, that's all you are. Oh yes, I've heard all about you, Mavis Dooley *and* Gwen Hinch!' She jumps to her feet. 'You, Mavis, are weird anyway and as for you, Gwen – well, everyone knows you're the town bike!' she screams, spit sprayin out the woman's gob like a lawn sprinkler.

'Fucken cunt! I fucked him. I fucked him. Geddit! Geddit! I done fucked ya husband!' Gwen yells as she charges at her. They land on the floor in a heap of legs and arms. Gwen has her down and starts pummelling into her chest.

Then from across the room Darryl pelts towards us, his face blood-red, his hands bunched into fists. 'Get off, get off!' he yells, knocking over bar stools as he rushes at us.

Terry throws down the pool stick, shoves Dotty aside and strides towards me. 'What's goin on, Mave?' he yells.

Ignoring him I turn round just as Darryl goes to put a steel capped boot into Gwen. *The fucken dog!* I charge at him and feel meself leave the floor for bout a second. I tackle him mid-section. The man's too grog-fucked to have a go back at a woman. He hits the ground with a thud.

'He tried to put the boot into Gwenny. What sorta man is he, eh? I ain't fucken takin that sorta shit!' I scream, then grab a handful of Darryl's hair and pull his head back. *Crackcrackcrackcrack.* His face caves in under me fists. *Take this, ya woman-bashin fucker.*

'Fuckin lemme go! Lemme go!' Darryl screams from under me as his hands beat the floor, like a little kid throwin a tantrum. *I want my mamma.*

Feelin satisfied I get up off him. Then I look round at the room. The bar is quiet n still as a morgue.

Everyone gapes at me an Darryl. Suddenly all the fellas point at Darryl and burst into loud laughter, a woman bashed the poor sucker, he must be piss weak, their looks say. I search the room for Gwenny. She stands in the corner crying, half her dress torn away and a large chunk of hair missing.

'You ever say a bad word bout her again n I'll come after you, Darryl Kane, ya got that!'

He glares at me, his shame complete. The rumble seems to have sobered him up; his mean, green eyes bore into me. 'I'll get you, Mavis Dooley, if it's the last thing I do,' he whispers, his voice cracked, as he lifts his bawlin, battered wife to her feet. I walk away feelin a small shiver a sorry for her. *Yep, Gwen kicked her arse!*

'Gwenny, I'm off home. You comin over for a drink?'

'Might as well.' She purses her lips.

'Don't worry bout it, girl.' I motion to the barmaid. 'Carton a Fourex.'

We walk out into the night. The carton a piss rests on me shoulders as we wobble towards my place.

'Thanks, Mave.' Gwen sniffles in the dark.

'S'all right, Gwenny. A woman weren't gonna let em kick ya when ya down. Ya ain't no fucken dog!'

'He'll do somethin to ya, Mave. Get revenge like. Ya shamejobbed the piss outta him, in front a his mates n all. A man, any man, ain't gonna be forgettin that too soon. Ya pulled away his big cock hero image.' Gwen sounds scared.

'Yep, well, a woman's been chased all her life. Ain't gonna make no difference to me,' I say, all gammon. I hear his words echoin inside me head: *I'llget youI'llgetyouI'llgetyouI'llgetyou.*

9

He's Comin Out

'Nevil, are ya gonna wake up to yerself n get down to the footy trainin whit the Blackouts?' I slam the carrot cake down on the table.

'Mum, I ... I just don't know if I want to play.' He throws Trevor a curious look.

'Don't wanna play! What sorta talk is that?'

'I – um, just don't think I can any more.' He drops his head.

'He's sick of it, Missus Dooley,' Trevor interrupts, his eyes meetin mine.

'Ohr, I get it. So this is your idea, Trevor?'

'No, no, it's not.'

'Seems mighty funny to me that Nev was doin okay til you come along. This ain't the city, Trevor. Kids like Nevil ain't got that *sophistikation* you fancy boys from the city got.' I slice into the cake.

'They'll be all right without me.' Nevil reaches cross to grab a hunk a cake.

'Bull. The Blackouts need ya, Nevie. What, yer gonna let em down now? Let poor ol Mum down. Yeah, that's right, Nevil, let poor ol Booty down? He so proud a ya, son. It'll kill him is what'll happen.' I plonk onto the chair n stare hard at him.

'Ain't letting anyone down. Mum, football's just a game, it's nothing to me! Fucking hell! There's more to life than throwing a ball across a bloody field. *Can't you see that!*'

'It's *everythin – you know that*! Ya got real talent, Nev. Ya could go places. Everybody knows you the best player round here, son. Yeah, Trevor, don't be givin me that look cos ya jus don't understand. I bet you never had to fight for anythin in ya life. This is the one chance for me boy to do somethin decent. To be a winner. Whatever ya gonna say, don't, cos it be nuthin to me. – So, Nevil, what ya want? To hang round the house playin dress up, is that it?' I give Trevor a look of disgust then I glare back at Nevil.

'*You just don't understand.* How can I ever tell you anything when you just don't want to listen. Yeah, that's right, Mum, you never listen to anything I tell you. I never wanted to play football. It was your dream. Yeah, Mum, your and Uncle Booty's dream, not mine. I always wanted to do something different. To be someone different. I can't be living a lie. Cos that's what it is. Yeah, Ma, a dirty big lie! I can do other things apart from football! It's just that you and Uncle could never really see.' He pauses. 'Ah, what's the point. You're never going to listen anyway.'

'Nev, don't say that. That's not true. I always listen.

And what the hell ya mean, ya wanna be different! What sorta talk is that! I just don't know ya any more, son. It's like somebody else comed along n took the real Nevil away.'

'It's true and you know it. You, Uncle Booty, all this town want me to be one thing and I never have any choice, do I? You set out to make me into the person *you* wanted me to be. Mum, times have changed. People have changed. I've always wanted to be like this, but I couldn't never, ever.' He stops and looks at me, suddenly his eyes are tired and very old.

'It's because of Trevor, ain't it? Yeah, ya started all this Jean Rhys rot jus before he turned up. That's where all this shit started. Number one, Nevil, you're not a woman. Number two, ya not white. Number three, football is ya only way outta this town.

'Number four, me n Uncle Booty doin our best for ya, son. We don't want you to end up like everybody else round here. That's right, drinkin piss, strung out on dope n knowin nuthin bout nuthin. Like all the other fellas in this friggin town, this country – yeah, they got deadly talent but they all gotta get out there n make their dreams come true. Fuck every other wanker that says ya can't do it cos I know ya can. I want ya to have everythin I didn't, son.' I stop and look over the boy's face. 'Ya gotta believe ol Mum on that one.' I twist me hands into a knot. *I don't know what else to say. How to tell him it's wrong to be wantin to be a woman. Havin mad, crazy ideas that no one gonna like. Havin to fight the town for him. Last, how hard*

119

it is for any black fella, let alone one thinkin he's some dead white sheila.

I slam me hands to me forehead. *That's his problem, don't wanna listen to common sense. Got his head stuck up in the friggin clouds. The boy's like the weakest kitten in the litter. Ain't got a hope less the mother be protectin it from everythin else. I know bout things like that n how they can fuck ya life up. I seen people like that. Ain't worth it sometimes. The runt'll always be different to others, weaker, that a truth.*

'Missus Dooley, may I say something?' Trevor asks, raisin one hand in the air like the man's in a classroom.

'Yeah?' I offer me best frown but feel meself runnin outta steam fast.

'Nevil is not like them – Big Boy, Grunta and the rest. He already has a special talent.' He pauses and looks at Nev. 'You see, what I'm trying to say is that Nevil doesn't belong here.' He turns to me and his eyes are sayin that he's not gonna back down.

'What the hell is this kinda talk! He doesn't belong here? Jeesus Christ, where *does* he belong, Trevor?' I tear the carrot cake into tiny pieces.

'Some place where he can find himself. Where he can be who he really is.'

I laugh and laugh. 'Find himself!' I splutter, carrot cake flyin outta me mouth.

'See. Just what I told you.' Nevil turns to Trevor and shrugs.

Trevor looks at me like I just pissed on his leg. His face suggests there's no hope here in this town, in this house, in me. He whispers somethin into Nevil's ear but Nevil shakes his head, no, no. Finally, I stop laughin n look at each a them in turn. For a fraction of a second I see a look flicker cross Nevil's face. A look I never saw before. Hopelessness. He's pissed off real bad.

So now I'm the big bad egg here. What's a woman sposed to do? Trevor talkin high-up shit into Nev's ear, I jus bet. Puttin stuff in there he got no right to. That's the problem whit Nevie, always listenin to other fellas steada me n his uncle. Ain't like he'll ever do anythin good as playin footy. Nah, nope, no dice. Sometime a woman gotta wonder, how could a kid like Nev boy turn out like this? Maybe Booty was right, that Nevil was always like this n I jus never seen it. Ahhh, a woman tryin her best.

I look at his made-up face, his painted fingernails and me ol floral house dress stretched tight cross his hairy chest. *It's not right. Where'd I go wrong?*

'Nevil, go n get dressed, son. Trevor, you shut ya mouth. I'm almost done whit the pair of ya. If ya any sorta mate you'd help Nevil out, talk some sense into him. Instead a feedin him whit fuckery ideas n shit. I oughta kick ya arse right outta this house. Ya jus member that I be watchin every move ya make, Trevor Wren Davidson! Any trouble here n I'll go straight cross that road there n bring Booty back, unnerstand?' I look at both of em. 'On your toes, Nevil.'

'What, Why? Where are we going?' He looks up at me, eyes slitted, angry.

'Doctor Chin. That's right D-O-K-T-E-R C-H-I-N-N. He can have a look at that head a yours.

Seems like there ain't nuthin us fellas round here know. Maybe the *doctor* will know what's wrong whitcha. Person oughta take you to see him too, Trevor.' I push the chair back under the table n stand whit me hands on me hips. 'Move it. Come on, Nevil, none a ya shit today. A woman jus ain't got the heart to be pissin bout any more.'

'Gee, Mum. Nah, I'm not going anywhere. Do you think I'm fucking loony, do you?' His face twists grey with anger.

'I know you're not mad,' I lie. *Worse thing in the world, tell a madman he's mad. Course he's gonna deny it. Like askin an alkie if he's a drunk. Nah, the dice don't roll that way.*

'Missus Dooley, I think you'd better sit down so I can explain things to you.' Trevor gets to his feet.

'Righto, if you can tell me what's goin on here I sure would preciate it. Trevor, I don't wanna hear any shit talk, either.' I pull out the chair, again, and sit.

He begins, 'Well, see, it's like this ...' and pauses as Booty strides into the room.

'How ya goin, son.' Booty greets him with a hard slap cross the back.

'G-good,' Trevor splutters, the wind knocked outta him.

Booty jabs a hairy finger in the air. 'Nevil, get that fucken shit off your face before I wipe it off meself.'

'I don't have to. You're not my boss, Uncle,' Nevil hurls over his shoulder, then makes a quick dash outta the room.

'Don't be too hard on him, Boot. He's not hisself.'

'Yeah, you can say that again,' Booty growls, then pulls up a chair n sits down next to Trevor. 'Listen, son, I gotta deal for you. Wanna make a few bucks?'

'Make some money, how?' Trevor coughs nervously, and looks at Booty with a slight frown. *Yeah, the boy is suss.*

'Boxin. Yeah, me n the boys got a ring set up down at the dog shed. Now, this fella you gonna fight is from Bullya, real mad fucka. I reckon you could take him out, whatcha reckon?' Booty smiles and cracks his knuckles.

'Me boxing! Oh gee!' Trevor gasps.

I wave me hand. 'Booty, come on now. Leave him be whit this mad shit.'

'Five hundred bucks is ridin. Big Boy n Grunta are in, so we need another fella. I nominated you, Trevor.' Booty laughs, his big gut wobblin as he turns in his chair n opens the fridge door. 'Any beer, Mave?'

'Behind the meat.' I watch Trevor. He don't look too flash. Matter a fact he look like he gonna spew up, his face sorta green n grey like.

'I can't do that. Oh no—' Trevor begins, but Booty cuts him dead.

'Here, get this into ya.' He shoves the beer at him. 'Mongrel Brandon, that's who we got lined up for you.' Booty grins.

'Mongrel?' Trevor whispers, his hands shakin as he tries to lift the cap on the beer.

'Crazy fucka.' Booty sighs whit respect. 'Now, he's got a good right hook so what you got to do is dodge that fucka cos if he lands one on you, Sonny Boy, then you'll be fucked good n proper. But I reckon you gotta good chance a layin him out. All the Bullya boys'll be there. I'll be takin on Reggie Drayden, that weak piss.' Booty takes a gulp of beer.

'I – I suppose you're using gloves? Boxing gloves to protect your hands?' Trevor asks, his voice thin.

'Gloves, ha!' Booty laughs. 'No fucken gloves here, my boy! She all bare knuckles. Ain't no pussy ever fought bare knuckles, eh.' He slaps Trevor on the shoulder.

'Look, um, I can't.' Trevor's lips quiver as he reaches cross the table n picks up the bottle opener. He rips the cap off n takes a big swallow.

'Shit. Don't talk shit, son. Your name's already down. If you don't turn up then the fight'll be in the backyard here, right?' Booty burps loud.

'I've got no choice, huh?' Trevor's eyelids flicker. He glances my direction.

'Yeah, ya have. Let him alone, Booty. If the boy don't wanna fight em mad bastards let him be. Ain't like Trevor knows bout that stuff.' I shove a piece a cake into me mouth and chew.

'Got Nev lined up whit Mad Dog Whitton. Nev'll bust his gut for sure.' Booty throws me a careful look.

'Ya got Nevil lined up to fight?' *Has he gone off his head?* 'But, Booty, Nevil don't know how to fight, not like that mob.'

'Get over it, Mavis. That's the problem whit him, too much sookyin up. He needs to get round whit men,

124

not women. Yeah, that's parta the problem, gettin round here all a time whit you, *a woman*. That's probly why the boy's thinkin he's a sheila!'

'Don't ya start on me, Booty Dooley! I'm his mother! Nevil put that idea in his own head bout bein a woman! Ya can't blame me for it. No way!'

'Yeah, well, tamarra night I want this fella n Nevil at my place. In the dog shed. Mavis, you keep away, it ain't no place for a woman to be. If Nevil don't turn up I'm gonna come here n drag his arse cross there, got it? You too, Trevor.' Booty gets to his feet. 'Five hundred bucks is ridin on you, boy. I spect you to knock this fucka off. Come over later n I'll teach you a few tricks – I know Mongrel's style, okay?'

Trevor, unable to open his mouth, looks up at Booty with a look of real terror, like he's gonna faint dead away. Knowin Booty's on a roll I keep me mouth shut til he walks outta the room. *Yeah, can't tell the bullhead anythin. Not that he'd really listen to me anyway.*

'Missus Dooley, I can't do that.' Trevor places the beer on the table, his hands shakin.

'You not the only one. Nev can't do that neither. I'll think a somethin. Ain't havin em Bullya boys tearin Nev to pieces.'

I swallow the last piece a cake n stand up. 'Been a long day. I might go n have forty winks, eh.'

'I'll go and have a talk to Nevil,' Trevor says, walkin to the sink whit the empty beer bottle. Suddenly he freezes on the spot, starin out the window.

'Trevor, ya right there?'

He turns to face me, unable to answer, n points out the window. I go cross n look out.

'Jesus God! Shit! Trevor, run down n tell Nev to get dressed proper. In his own clothes!' I grab the bottle outta his hand n push him towards the hall. 'Hurry up!'

I turn back to the window.

Big Boy has Grunta up on his shoulders n all the Blackouts are followin him through the front gate, singin and yellin: 'The Nev. We want the Nev. Weee want the Nev.'

Suddenly, from the opposite side a the street, Gracie tears cross the road like she's got fire up her arse and joins em. *Yeah, a woman jus can't win no matter which way ya slice it.*

I go to the front door, me heart thuddin whit fear. *Can only hope Nev got outta that dress bloody fast.* I swing the door wide open.

'Hey, hey, Missus D, we want the Nev,' Grunta shouts down at me from his perch.

I look past them at the rest a the crew. Some sit on the lawn; others haunch down on their legs watchin me, then watchin the door. *Could they know? Maybe Dotty already tole em all bout Nevie. Gee, it never ends! And Gracie – well, she looks like she's ready for the morgue. The girl fulla dope.*

'Gracie, what's goin on?'

'Nuthin, Mum. I just comed across to see Nev is all.' She can't look me in the eye.

'Nev, we want the Nev,' they chant.

'All right, just shut up, will youse. Wait there n I'll get him.' I swing round but as I do, I notice Missus Warby on her kero tin. She don't look happy.

'An uprising, Mavis!' she shouts across at me.

'Somethin like that,' I answer as I go into the house.

Trevor comes down the hallway shakin his head n mutterin to hisself.

'Where is he? They're waitin out the front. I can't keep em there all day!' I feel a pain in me chest. A tight ache.

'He doesn't want to see them. He won't come out of his room.' Trevor bites on his bottom lip.

'Shittin hell, that's all a woman needs!' I push past him to the bedroom, me legs move like they wadin through mud.

Nevil lays back on his bed propped up whit two pillows. The room stinks, marijuana smoke races up my nose. For a second I feel light-headed, head startin to spin.

'Nevil, get up! They're out there waitin for ya! Come on!' I plead, me mouth all spitted out.

'I don't care. Let them stand there all day if they like,' he says with a wild laugh.

He's high. Yep, off his scone.

'Jus go out n see em for a minute. That can't hurt, can it?' I run a hand cross me forehead, me head throbs.

'Okay, just this once.' Nevil gets up and goes towards the door.

'Hey! Out of em bloody clothes first! Ya not goin out there like that!'

He drops his shoulders, then laughs and makes his way to the bathroom. I run back down the hall. *Oohhhh, me blood pressure's risin like a loaf a bread in a oven.*

'Trevor, make sure he gets dressed proper.' I tap him on the shoulder then go puffin n gaspin to the front door. *Cool down. Steady up, ol woman. Slap a smile on ya dial n smooth it over.*

By this time Grunta is tacklin Big Boy on the grass. Gracie looks like she's had nough piss n dope to sink a ship. And the rest have a half-empty carton of beer in front a them. Missus Warby stands on her kero tin but her attention is glued on the footballers. Feelin I owe her an explanation I go over to the fence. *Yep, she'll get a few good yarns outta this. What will it be this time – drugs, grog, gamblin?*

She watches me whit slitted eyes as I stand before her. 'Hello there,' I greet her in my best suckin up voice.

'A riot. That's what you'll have on your hands, Mavis. Never was one to condemn anyone, but that mob there look mighty stirred up. Drunk half of them and that girl there – well, she looks like she needs a good sleep. Gracie Marley, isn't it? Yes, I thought so. Some people will just put up with anything and they feel they can't ask for help – but Mavis, I'm here.' She purses her lips and offers a look of pity.

'Oh, they harmless. The footy team, the Blackouts. They jus waitin for Nev to come out.' I grin weakly.

'As I've said again and again, I've looked after many folk around these parts. I've been a pillar of strength to those that can't handle things that life throws at them. You don't have to feel you're not good enough for me, Mavis Dooley. I can see you have a lot of trouble over there. I've been here for years and have always had great respect for you and Nevil.' She shakes her grey head firmly.

'No, it's okay. Really ain't no trouble, Missus Warby. Kids'll be kids, eh?' I give a small con job laugh. *Biggest load a shit ever comed outta a woman's gob.*

'Kids, huh. They're grown men. Now, if you'd like me to tell them to get off your property—' she offers hopefully, her wrinkled face alight.

I'm bout to answer when I hear the Blackouts shoutin and laughin crazy like. *That's a good sign.* Whit this thought I turn and look at the doorway. *That's it, I'm finished.*

Me eyes travel from his sandshoe-clad feet, jeans-clad legs, and a fringed cowboy shirt half-open to the waist. Finally, me eyes rest on his face. Nevil looks like he's a walkin advertisement for Avon. Bright red lipstick smeared cross his lips, green eyeshada on his eyelids, brick-red rouge circled round his cheekbones. One hand clutches me ol handbag. *Nnnnnooooooooo!* Me legs wobble, I struggle to keep breathin, fling an arm out an grab hold a the fence.

Trevor stands behind Nev, grinnin n pale-faced as he waves at everybody on the lawn.

'Dear Lord!' Missus Warby gasps.

I don't say anythin. I can't say anythin. Me jaw feels

like it's clamped whit barbed wire. Me hands shake like they got a life a their own, me heart beats so hard n fast that for a instant I feel like I might have a heart turn. Then as if on cue Booty strides through the gate, pig dogs in tow.

At first he doesn't see Nevil on the step. He just looks at me then follows me wide and horrified eyes. Then he spots him.

Bein the fast thinker he is, Booty walks towards the Blackouts and yells, 'Who's gonna take out the game! Whose gonna whop them fuckas!' He throws a large, hairy fist into the air.

Circlin the lawn like a pair a scabby-coated vultures, the pig dogs, eyes pissin yella n muzzles white whit drool, bark n howl.

Big Boy and Grunta hold their stomachs as they point and laugh at Nevil.

'Crazy prick,' Big Boy chokes out.

'A sheila! A pussy!' Grunta howls.

'The Blackouts! Number one! Yahoooooo!' Nevil screams, throwin his arms high in the air. He steps out onto the lawn and grabs a beer off someone.

'Was always the one for a joke, eh Missus D?' Big Boy yells, salutin me whit a bottle a beer.

'That's me Nev!' I shout back with as much enthusiasm as I can muster. *Close call. Friggin close. They all think he's jokin. They think it's a big laugh, gee.*

Booty struts round doin his best tough-fella act while throwin Nevil real deadly looks. The pig dogs, all barked n howled out, crouch back gainst the fence, scarred ears pricked for master's orders.

Sittin on the step, drinkin beer, shovin a joint in his mouth n laughin up is Trevor. *Probably so nerve-wracked he needs it.*

I pass Gracie. 'Mum, ain't he loony, eh?' She points at Nevil, who by now is surrounded by team mates.

'More n you know,' I mumble, then go inside and make a fast dash to the kitchen window.

Missus Warby motions Booty towards her and I watch as her mouth moves ten to the dozen. *Geez, a woman can't take any more a this.*

I slam the window shut and go into the lounge room. I flick the TV on. Ricki Lake laughs loud and clear. 'That's life.' She smiles, real satisfied.

10

Bare Knucklin

Chad Morgan croons loud and miserable from the stereo speakers; cars are parked cross every centimetre a yard. People lay back on the grass drinkin, smokin yarndi n placin bets as the sun goes down. They're all geared up for the knucklin.

The Blackouts huddle together in a tight knot at the side a the shed, talkin n laughin. *They're here for me boy. Jus hope he don't let em down. Anythin could come a this. Me boy is their hero – n sometimes heroes get their arses kicked. A woman reckons this is gonna happen here tonight.*

Booty strolls out of the doorway shirtless, shoeless, holdin a notepad and a beer. He walks round talkin to people and scribblin into his book. He looks hyped-up.

'Think a somethin, Gwenny.' I nudge her in the ribs as we stand hidden behind the bushes.

'I'm thinkin, woman. Jus settle down n don't panic. You'd think Booty'd have more sense, wouldn't ya. He's womba, Mave, that what the man is. Mad.' She hauls a beer outta the box at our feet.

'Should never have let em come over. That bloody

Booty, I'm gonna do him over tamarra if it's the last thing a woman do. Yeah, ya right, he mad. But ya know I can't tell him anythin.' *Oh no, Booty's always right.* I pull back the branches and peer into the near darkness.

'Mavis, look! There, over there in the corner.' Gwen points to the lit up shed.

'Shittin hell! Who's that?' I feel me teeth ache as I take in the tall, wide, muscle-packed figure flexin his arms as he stands before Booty. *He's a man that seed plenty a dry creekbeds. Lookin at him tells me that. A man that uses his fists for fun. Yep, jus the type Booty gets along whit. Painin for the thrill a it. Hurtin young fellas, that be his game. Yep, Mavis Dooley can spot a wile horse ten feet away, n this ol brumby be rearin at the bit.*

'That's Mongrel Brandon from Bullya. He plays for the Rammers. Jeesus Christ, get a load of them arms! Oowwhh, Mave, reckon I don't like this much,' Gwen whispers, her voice crackin.

'Friggin hell! Trevor can't fight that!' *Oh, Trev.* I stand up to get a better look.

'Get ya arse down, Mave! They'll see ya.' Gwen yanks on the hem a me dress.

I crouch back down in the bushes n peer out through the leaves. *Booty'll bust his guts if he see us here. Do his block good n proper.*

'They're going in!'

I jump up. 'Could we like sneak up the side a the shed n watch from there?'

'Righto, let's run cross.' Gwen starts to move out,

then suddenly freezes. 'Listen for a minute. Mave, do you hear anything in that bush over there? Shh, shh, hear it? Like somethin's movin,' she whispers then takes small careful steps forward and peers hard into a nearby bush.

I look into the darkness but can't see anything. Suddenly I hear the shakin of branches real close. 'Somebody's here, Gwen,' I whisper, mouth dry.

'I jus knew it would be bad luck to come here spyin,' Gwen sounds ready to give up.

'Who's there? Come out,' I growl, in me loudest don't-fuck-round-whit-me voice.

The bush rustles near Gwen and with one fast move and a yelp the branches part and out steps a figure. I stumble back, fear racin up me spine.

'Fucken hell!' Gwen squeals out. Tryin to keep her balance she grabs hold a the nearest gum tree but misses and ends up on her arse in the burrs. 'Jeesus Christ!'

'Mum? Mum Dooley, is that you?' Gracie's broken voice fills the darkness.

'Gee, gee Gracie whatcha doin, girl?' I follow the sound of her voice.

'Thought I'd come and have a gawk at the fight. Booty barred women from comin,' she says, keepin her voice low.

'Why didn't you say you were there? Scared the fuck right outta us, Gracie,' Gwen snaps as she gets to her feet.

'I didn't even know youse was here til Gwen came up and looked in the bush here. Don't shit yaself, Gwenny. I been sittin there for bout an hour now. Didn't want

Booty to suss on me. I knew what was goin on – Brayden Mengel told me yesterday. Reckoned Nevil was gonna get a floggin good and proper. I jus had to come over n check it out.'

'Look, love,' I wheeze, me breath catchin back, 'we gonna go over to the side of the shed n see if we can get a better look. Booty's got Nev lined up whit some Mad Dog from Bullya.' I grab her by the arm and steer her up the fence line.

'But Nev can't fight. We all know that.'

'That's why I'm here. Ain't no Mad Dog gonna hurt my boy!' I grind me teeth. *Bare knucklin, eh. Nev couldn't fight his way outta brown paper bag. N Trevor, well, he easy meat no matter which way ya look at it. Geez, if I'd a known it was gonna all come to this ... Nah, violence no good for young fellas like em. It won't make Nev a man, it'll only get him a broken nose or worse.*

'Gwenny, you see anythin? Spot Nevil or Trevor anywhere?' I watch her back as she peeks round the shed corner.

'Fucken Jeesus! Mave, come here quick!' She moves across and I stand beside her. 'Look at that!' she gasps, pointin inside.

Fellas sit on empty drums, on the dirt, some sit on their haunches, others stand round a wide circle drawn in the dirt n roped off with two strands of thick twine. The ring. Booty's boxin ring.

On one side a the room sit four men, one of em Mongrel. But it's not Mongrel me eyes are drawn to. Seated at the far end is a short, squat, almost bald-headed man. It's only when he stands up that me gut turns to water. He's built to demolish. His pump-iron arms ripple as he moves them back n forth. Legs like a side a beef. Head like one a Booty's dogs n a face that'd turn milk sour. Runnin from his shoulder blade to the tips a his fingers is a snake tattoo and the words: *Death and Glory.*

I take a small step back into the dark when I see Booty walk towards him. 'Mad Dog, ya prick!' Booty greets him whit a hard slap cross the back.

'Oh,' I groan, then holdin onto my stomach I turn to Gwen and Gracie. 'Nev's sposed to fight *him*!' I whisper, a roar startin somewhere in the back a me skull, me heart beats so fast it leaves me breathless, feelin light-headed n sick I wanna kill Booty here n now. Gwen and Gracie look round the corner where I point.

'Nah. Booty wouldn't let Nev fight him, Mave?' Gwen wrinkles her brow.

'Nev can't fight anybody! Nevil couldn't fight me little sister! Why Booty gotta get Nev into all this?' Gracie hisses, soundin fired up.

'Think a somethin. Maybe we should jus barge in,' I offer.

'Don't panic jus yet. Wait and see what happens.' Gwen puts the stubbie to her mouth.

I take another look, sweepin the room whit me eyes. Draggin his bare feet in the dust, sweat beadin his lip n hair plastered to his scalp, Nevil shuffles slowly to the ring. Me gut heaves n clenches, I eyeball the crowd for Booty. Then I spot him, struttin into the centre a the ring. Holdin up one hairy arm he bellows, 'Here in the right corner ...'

I look round the room and see, with disbelief, Trevor walkin out from a dark corner. No shirt, no shoes. He looks dead already. His hair falls cross his baby face, his eyes red n puffed n his legs look like they gonna seize up at any minute. *The boy ain't gonna do too well here tonight. By rights, he oughta drop dead right there on the spot.*

I feel so bad n sorry for him that I promise if anybody gonna be punchin him bout I'll be the one standin in front a him. Ain't right, young fella like him. Wouldn't ever have seen stuff like this in his life. These ol backyard boys been fightin since they could walk. They born that way. Trevor don't have no chance here. He's in wrong territory.

'Mum, look at Nev!' Gracie hits me on the arm.

'Gee, Mave, it don't look too good.' Gwen sidles up beside me.

Nevil dances, prances and skips round the ring, arms windmillin in all directions as Mad Dog throws a few lefts n rights at him. Booty starts yellin, 'That's it Boy. Watch that fucka! Keep your head down, son.'

Nevil is startin to look sick n scared as he moves round dodgin Mad Dog's callused knuckles as they drive in closer to his face.

Trevor sits on the molasses tin holdin a beer, watchin

Nevil, bitin on his bottom lip so hard I see small dots of blood appear.

Booty starts circlin the ring, throwin his fists in all directions and screamin at Nevil to take Mad Dog down. 'Kill the fucka! Get him, get him!' he rages. *Bloodlust.*

With one short, sharp jab, Mad Dog catches Nevil on the chin and sends him flyin backward with such force the noise of him hittin the dirt reaches me ears.

'Take that, you fuckin queen!' Mad Dog roars at Nevil, then standin over him he puts the boot into his guts.

Nevil, sweat pissin down his face, blood runnin down his chin, tries to get to his feet when *whack*! Mad Dog puts him back on his arse.

I see red. That Mad Dog fucker! Hittin me boy like that! Whitout thinkin I burst into the ring, screamin, fists flyin as I charge towards Mad Dog. *Hittinmeboyhittinmeboybastardbastardbastard!* I feel the crowd fall back away. I hear laughter, hoots n above all Booty yellin: 'Mavis, get back! I doned fucken tole you, woman!'

Suddenly in that wild moment I meet Mad Dog's black eyes. They fly wide open. His mouth drops, like the man can't believe what he sees.

'Ya leave me son alone! Hear that! Leave Nevil alone! I'll do ya over!' I bust me guts full force. Then I'm flyin through the air. Booty's arms are wrapped round me waist, pullin me back.

'Keep goin, boys!' he yells as he hauls me off to the back a the crowd. 'Settle down, Mave. Come on, Sis, he ain't gonna get hurt. I tole ya not to come here,' he spits.

'Bullshit, he killin him, Boot. He gonna kill him!' I struggle to free myself from his arms.

'Mavis, shut up and listen! Nev got more guts than any one here! He'll prove himself, Mave. He don't need you comin in shamin the fuck outta him. This is man's business. I fucken tole ya to *stay away*!' Booty shouts in me face.

It's then I know that I've gone and done it; me brother ain't never yelled me down in all a me life. I feel vomited.

'Just sit down n shut up. Whatcha think, I'm gonna let Mad Dog hurt him, eh?'

I can't keep me trap shut now, things gettin right outta control. I swing on him. 'Ya better not! Nevil gets hurt in there then that's it, ya not gonna be me brother no more. That's right, Booty, I'll wipe me hands of ya. I'll never talk to ya again! I fucken mean it!' I collapse down on the dirt, out of breath n feelin gut sick. *It's all Booty's fault this business. N there no need for him to be shoutin at a woman like that.*

Booty returns to the ring. I spot Gracie n Gwen sneakin along the side wall.

'Sit down.' I pat the ground. 'Things don't look too flash. I jus told Booty that if anyone hurt me boy I'm never gonna talk to him again. Booty's tryin to make Nev somethin he's not. Nev'll never be like em fellas. A woman wouldn't want him to be.' We turn back to the ring as Booty yells, 'Round Two!'

Nevil steps back into the circle, breathin like he got

asthma, swollen eyes snaked down, chin gashed wide open, chest sportin cuts n bruises. *He's taken a floggin. He'll go down any minute now. Any minute. A woman should get in there n get that Dog before he murders the boy.*

Mad Dog jumps into the circle n starts dancin round Nevil. 'Mummy boy. Can't fight ya own battles? *Yeaaahhh*, little motherfucker,' he taunts with loud bursts of laughter, throwin fists at the crowd.

The crowd love it. They start chantin: 'Maddogmaddogmaddogmaddogbusthimbusthim!'

I cast a look towards Booty but he ignores me and watches the ring whit hooded eyes n tight mouth.

Trevor spots me, lookin sideways, he creeps behind the mob to plonk himself down next to me.

'Gee, Missus Dooley, he's killing Nevil. Maybe we should ask Booty to cancel it, what do you think?' he asks, wringing his hands and lookin like he wants to curl up into the dirt.

'Son, Booty'd rather die n call this off.' I watch as Nevil moves round the ring. This time he moves whit more cunning, bobbin n weavin as Mad Dog's fists search for a hit.

Mad Dog weaves, struts n jumps round the ring like he's some sorta Anthony Mundine. Sweat rolls down his face and runs into his eyes, his knuckles piss blood as he punches em into Nevil's face.

'Dodge him, dodge him, son!' I scramble to my feet, screamin.

'In the guts. That fucken big gut a his!' Gwen yells.

'Put him down, lovey!' Gracie's voice louder n everybody else's, so that the men in front a us turn round and give us a look like we just called em a dirty name.

'You women want to get outta here,' one of them snaps at us.

I ignore him and concentrate on Nevil's steady form. *The boy like one of em ballerina dancers. Yeah, probably a good thing like.*

Mad Dog offers Nevil a big, smirkin grin n says real loud, 'I fucked ya mother.'

I hear it but before it sinks in, Booty strides out fast towards me and holds my arms down. 'Settle down, Sissy. He's tryin to rile Nev up. It's gammon. He's tryin to get Nevil stirred up is all.'

Then it jus happens me – Nevil isn't me Nevil any more. The yella-faced fella in the ring ain't me boy. He swings hisself round on one foot, his face raged. His whole body look like it growed up from nowhere. He's a lunatic.

Mad Dog takes a step back. Not fast enough. Nevil drives at him like a big whirly wind comin in off the dry flats. His fists fly with such speed, so deadly that it takes a second to realise they are Nevil's fists. Mad Dog don't have a hope.

His punches split open Mad Dog's face like a watermelon. Everything falls in on him, his nose squashes back, his lips twist to one side a his face, his eyes bulge, as he hits the ground with a whump. He don't move. *Me boy busted him good. I see Mad Dog in bad pain. Good job.*

141

Nevil stands over him and looks down. 'No one talks about my mother that way. You piece a fucken garbage. Next time I'll kill you!' He spits it out then walks from the ring, his shoulders bruised n straight.

Somewhere inside a me I can't take it all in. Me boy ain't a boy any more. He's somebody to be reckoned whit. Booty lets go a me arms. 'I knew he'd lift him,' he says. 'Nev got more guts than any a us will ever know.' He walks away, his chest puffed out.

I stare after him, not believin my ears. *He* was always the one sayin Nevil was a pussy!

'Missus Dooley, can you tell Booty I don't want to fight?' Trevor hangs off me arm. Someone will have to pry him off.

'You don't have to, son.' I reach across and pat him on the back, just as Booty returns with Mongrel Brandon.

'You up next. Move ya arse, I got money ridin on ya, Sonny Jim.' Booty grabs Trevor by the arms and pulls him from me.

'Missus Dooley, please explain to him. Missus Dooley, tell him! Mister Booty, I can't fight, I don't know how to!' he shouts, as Booty pushes him towards the ring.

'Too late for that, Sonny. Ya gotta go whit ya instincts. Do what I tell ya and ya'll be right.' Booty shoves him. I go to say somethin, but right then I see Nevil comin towards me.

'Did all right, eh?' he asks, a bright smile on his busted face.

'Sorta hoped ya would. Ya did well, son. But you

better do somethin bout poor ol Trevor. Mongrel'll bust the boy a new face.' I point to the ring.

Trevor sits on the ground, his head between his knees as Mongrel towers over him shoutin, 'Get up, white boy!'

Bringin his head up, Trevor gets to his feet n falls backwards on wobbly legs, his hands coverin his face as he peers out through his fingers.

'Don't fuck about! Trevor, get him! Show him whatcha made a, boy!' Booty yells, runnin in n outta the ring, tryin to shove Trevor towards Mongrel.

'Please, mate, I don't want to fight. I don't,' Trevor pleads. Then just as Mongrel rushes in at him, something happens. I hear the noise first, dogs yelpin and barkin, then spotlights blaze in the doorway. It's a bust.

Everyone runs towards the back door, screamin, 'Gungies! Fucken cops! The purrleecce. Boys in blue! The boys in blue!' The mob scatters in all directions. Some cut it through the back door, others chance the front. I swivel round on me feet and look about for the boys. In the corner I spot me Nev. I grab him by the arm and steer him out the back door then race back in to grab the others. But as I eyeball the room I can't find Trevor anywhere.

'Trevor, Trevor! Son, where ya at? Gotta move your butt, boy, the cops're here!' I yell into the now empty room. No one answers. I feel a sickness in the bottom a me gut. *Trevor's disappeared.*

Back in the bushes we stand watchin as Booty is led off by the copper, Max Brown, and shoved into the back of the gungie cab. Then, as one of the police cars speed past I catch a glimpse of Trevor, screamin wordlessly as he tries to claw his way out through the back window. I keep watchin as the cop car speeds off into the night.

Oh no, not Trev. I groan. *Of all the people in the shed, they had to haul his sorry arse off. What sorta luck does that to a boy like him?*

Feelin gut sick n weary we all head back to my place, Gwen's swearin about all coppers. Nevil, head bent, walks along as though he's lost in his own world. Gracie walks behind him. 'Couldn't do much more, Nevil. No one would expect that. Ya done what ya could.' She reaches out n grabs hold a his hand.

Gwen walks up beside him. 'Ya gotta do what ya gotta do. Don't worry, love, Big Boy'll be proud of ya.'

'It's done, no use worryin bout it now. Nevil, ya done whatcha had to, son. But, tell me somethin, how'd ya know to fight like that?'

'Could always fight like that, Ma. Ya think I survived this long without knowing how to look after myself? I got the best teacher in the world. Yeah, that's right – *you*, old girl.' He finds a laugh.

'Seemed a woman did somethin right.' I watch Nevil's back n wonder where this fella come from. Wonder what goes on in that head a his. *Seems like I never did know the boy to start whit.*

11

The Dealer

Max Brown looks at me over his wire-rimmed glasses. 'Do you know who he really is?' he asks, shufflin papers.

'Yeah, I know who he is,' I reply, pattin down the hem a me dress.

'I don't think you do,' he answers with a short laugh.

'Well, if he ain't Trevor Davidson, who is he?' I watch Max's face redden.

'I shouldn't tell you this, Mavis, but that bloke in there isn't Trevor Davidson.' He pauses, his dull grey eyes takin in the shocked look on me face. 'His real name is Isaac Edge. That's right, the biggest drug dealer this side of the dingo fence,' he says, pointin in the direction of the cells.

'Isaac Edge! Ya gotta be jokin!'

'No joke, Mavis. That's one tough bastard in there. Don't be fooled by that pretty boy face of his. He's a killer. Yep, done more time than we ever had lunches. It just isn't safe for you to have anything to do with him.'

I stare at him tryin to find some flicker a mischief in his face. There ain't. *Max Brown never jokes, ever. The man's a vault.*

'How do you know he's Isaac Edge?' I question him.

'I got the detectives down here from Bullya. They've got an identikit. It's our man. Now, Mavis, if there's anything you want to tell me—' He coughs loudly and offers me a curious look.

'Like what?' I'm still disbelievin.

'Anything he may have told you or Nevil. Any mention of drugs – anything, really.'

'Done told me nuthin. Max, you got the wrong man! Trevor definitely ain't no big time drug dealer! That the craziest thing I ever heard.' I wipe the sweat off me lip. *Yep, Max getting too ol for this job.*

'That's his ace card, his smooth looks make an impression on women. Don't be taken in by that. You're not the first one he's fooled. That's how he operates, preying on innocent folk.' Max nods his head firmly, his lips curled back in disgust.

'I'd betcha my life he ain't no drug dealer. I jus don't swallow it.' I slap a smile on me dial, hopin that'll convince the man.

'Well, we caught him at your brother's place, bare-knuckle boxing. Doesn't that tell you something, hmm?'

'Wrong man, Max. I don't believe it. He's *Nevil*'s mate! No, I ain't seen anythin suss. The boy treat me house like a castle.'

'Look, Mavis, I hate to tell you this but he's our man. Perhaps it's true he's been very nice to you but that's just an act. Trust me, I know about this type of scum.'

'Anyway, can I go n see him?'

'If you want to, but be careful. He's a lot smarter than he lets on. Don't be taken in by his claims of innocence, Mavis. I know some folk from small towns are charitable and all the rest of it but this bludger is a parasite and he'll take advantage of you. Be on your toes, Missus Dooley.'

'Yeah, how he gonna take advantage of me, eh?' I laugh. *Take advantage of me! Trevor a big timer drug dealer! Not friggin likely.*

'Use you, Mavis,' Max says, dead certain.

'Can't see how. A woman ain't got nuthin he'd want.'

'Mavis, people like this are sleazebags and because I've known you for a long time I'm just trying to warn you to be careful. He's been selling stuff here in Mandamooka. I'm advising you in your best interests here. The problem is we get all the city scum coming out here trying to sell this rubbish to our kids. I won't have it!'

'Trevor's been sellin drugs? I mean, can you prove he's been sellin here?'

'We have witnesses. I just regret that he's taken advantage of your goodwill. That's the thing, Mavis, you're too good-hearted. But I can't tell you any more than this.' He grabs a big bunch a keys and stands up.

Trevor a drug dealer? Nah, jus don't add up, do it? Load a bulldust. Isaac Edge me arse. I let the thoughts go and follow Max to the cells.

Trevor sits on the edge of the cell bed, his head between his knees.

'Trev, love,' I say, and at the sound a me voice the boy leaps up.

147

'Missus Dooley, thank God! They're saying I'm some sort of drug dealer! That I'm selling drugs to kids and everything!' he blurts out, his face pasty, eyes red, his whole body tremblin. I go in and sit beside him.

'It's okay, Max. He won't do anythin.'

'Right, Mavis. I'll be just out here if you need me.' Max pushes the cell door closed with a loud clang.

Trev's voice is shaky. 'I've given them my business card and told them to phone Brisbane and check out my story.'

'They think you're some fella by the name a Isaac Edge. Trev, what's goin on? Now tell me the truth.'

Trevor turns to me with a look of desperation. 'There's nothing to tell. I haven't done a damned thing. Oh God, why me? Ever since I came to this bloody town I've had nothing but bad luck. Missus Dooley, you don't think I'm a drug dealer, do you?'

'Love, I know ya ain't. They jus got you mixed up whit this other fella that looks like you. But, I can't work out how the hell Max hauled ya in.'

'I think it was your neighbour and another woman. I walked past them both the other day when I was carrying my briefcase. I heard the old woman say to her friend: "Look, Dotty, it's the druggie boy." Like, you know, they thought I had the drugs in my briefcase!' He sighs wearily and stares down at the concrete floor.

'Friggin Missus Warby n Dotty Reedman! I shoulda guessed. Missus Warby's a real ol stickybeak n Dotty Reedman's the biggest liar this side a the black stump!

148

Jeesus, a woman can't friggin win!' I grit me teeth. *Don't it ever end?*

'How's Nev holding up?'

'Trevor, they only brought you in yesterday, not ten years ago!' I laugh. 'Nevil's fine. Righto, Trev, you wanna tell me once and for all what the hell's goin on whit you two. Things seemed to take a turn when you showed up. I wanna know right here, right now, what the fuckery's been goin on, hmmm?' *Danger question this one.*

'I can't really say. Um, well, I don't really know.' He shrugs his shoulders.

'Trevor, somethin's goin on whit you two. What is it? I ain't no idiot. I got eyes n see things.'

'Missus Dooley, I can't tell you. No, Missus Dooley, I'm not Nevil's boyfriend if that's what you think. It's all been some terrible mistake, all of this. It's like I walked into some sort of nightmare. I'm just here to help Nevil, that's all.'

'Help Nevil? What's that sposed to mean, eh?'

'He doesn't want me to tell you or anyone. Nevil's just not ready to tell you anything just yet. And as his friend I've sworn that I won't say anything. Please, Missus Dooley, please just be ... well ... be patient.'

'Be *patient*! Patient me foot! Ever since the day he woke up n said he's a woman there ain't nuthin been the same since! I reckon it's got a hell of a lot to do whit you.'

'Well, don't worry about me too much. I'll be going home after the football game. When Nevil's ready to tell you and everyone else what's going on, he will.'

'Yeah, I got a good idea a what's happenin. Ya want Nevil to go to the big smoke so he can be a transvestay! That's it, ain't it?' *Yep, this ol scrubber been round. I know the big timin city ways.*

He looks at me like I'd hit him whit a two-by-four. Then he laughs so hard that tears run down his cheeks. He doubles over n falls onto the floor, holdin his stomach as he gasps n splutters.

I realise the boy ain't right in the head. *He's mucked up, maybe from drugs? Come to think of it em eyes a his look kinda zonked out. Should get him to Doctor Chin.*

'Tranny. A tranny,' he gasps, gettin to his feet and holdin onto the dirty sink.

I jus sit n stare at him. *Can't work the fella out like. One thing for sure, he ain't no friggin Isaac Edge! Smooth, huh? He's bout as smooth as a friggin ride in the back a Booty's ute!*

'Nev a tranny. A tranny!' He collapses onto the bed and looks at me, red-faced and horrified at the same time. Like he can't stop hisself. Like he wanna stop laughin but everytime he look at me he gotta start up again.

'It's the drugs, ain't it?' I purse me lips. 'Tell me, Trevor. I know ya ain't no dealer but I know ya smoke it,' I whisper hoarsely. *Maybe he's fulla that arse drug – crack? I dunno why they'd wanna shove it up their ring holes for – it got a woman beat. Maybe this poor crapper fulla that shit? Yep, n maybe he got Nevil hooked on it?*

'Son, ya full a crack is ya?' I have to ask.

He coughs loudly, then clears his throat. 'Crack, Missus Dooley? Like drugs?' He flings back his head n looks at me like I'm the lunatic.

'That's right, Trevor. Crack, Mary Jane, drugs, dope, stuff that makes people think they somethin else. Yeah, make a man think he a woman.' *Chew on that.*

'My God! Absolutely not! Oh, Missus Dooley, I thought you knew me by now. How on God's earth did you come up with an idea like that?'

'Now, Trevor, I could be wrong but a mother has to keep her eyes peeled on her kid, right? If I found ya was givin me boy that sorta shit, then, son, ya ain't gonna be gettin outta this town alive.'

'Missus Dooley, you've got to believe me. I wouldn't, no, I don't do drugs. Never have! Nevil's not on anything, you must believe me! Please, oh please, believe me.'

'If I was you – Trevor, Isaac Edge, whoever the hell ya really are – I'd be more worried bout what em ol detectives are gonna do to ya. That's right, Trevor, detectives! They ain't here for a Sunday picnic, is they? Ooohhh nnooo, they're here to haul ya arse off to the big lockup.'

'What detectives? And for what?' he blabbers, face palin, hands shakin.

Yeah, that knocked the piss right outta him. Made the boy realise this is bad egg business we dealin whit.

'Cos they think ya Isaac Edge! Ya in big trouble, Sonny!' I watch his chin collapse onto his chest. *The boy wouldn't make a drug dealer's dog. Nah, he soft, soft as butter. I can see it in the back a his scared eyes. The boy ready to bawlbaby.*

'Tell them, Missus Dooley! Tell them I'm not that

person, for God's sake! I can prove it. Yeah, I can really prove it!' He stands up, his whole body quiverin like a fly-swarmed horse.

'I already done that. The only thing—' I stop as the cell door flings open and two navy-suited men stride in, Max Brown behind them. *The Ds.*

'Mavis, please step outside while the detectives have a talk to our friend here.' Max steers me out the door and into his office.

'Max, what's goin on?' I ask, a thick lump in me throat. *They gonna sew the boy up.*

'They need to ask a few questions. Look, I'm sorry, Mavis, that you've got to go through all this but it's my duty.' Max offers me a seat. 'Anyway, how's Nevil? Ready for the big game, is he?'

'He's all right. Yeah, he's lookin forward to the game. It's his life you know. I reckon we'll take it out this year, eh?'

'With Nevil playing we're bound to. Talented boy you got there, Mavis. All the more reason you got to keep him from scum like that in there.' Max hates druggies, full stop.

'Now Mavis, I've got a few phone calls to make. So you take yourself off home.' He shoos me outta his office and I pretend to head out the front door. I sidle up the side wall n cock me ear in the direction of the voices.

'That's right, Edge, cocaine.'

'Coke.'

'Nose candy.'

'You had it all set up, didn't you? Preying on the town people like a fucking vulture. Yeah, had it set from go, didn't you?'

'Fucking skag bucket.'

'No, no, sir, please, you've got it all wrong.'

'Yeah? How wrong can two deaths be?'

'We're gonna do you over, boy.'

'Bare knuckling, hey. Let's see how tough you are in the big house.'

'No, no ... I ... I'm not tough. No, sir, I can't.'

'Using Missus Dooley, aren't you? Nice lady like her. Using them pretty boy looks to suck her in. Fucking cocksucking bastard!'

'No! No! Please don't hit me! Sir, I respect Missus Dooley!' Trevor yells loud and squeaky.

Me heart races in terror as I flatten meself gainst the wall. *What can I do?*

Panic grips me. That friggin Dotty n Missus Warby, they cause all a this! Suddenly a piercin scream rips through the air. Goosebumps break out on me neck. *That's it. That's it. I've had nough a this shit! Can't they see he wouldn't hurt a fly.* I pelt through the cell door knockin the fat D outta the way.

'He's not fucken Isaac Edge! Hear that, not fucken Edge! Ya got it all wrong!' I shout wildly, more so when I see Trevor's tear-stained, terrified face. 'Leave him alone! Ya listenin to the biggest liars in town! Dotty Reedman's a liar. Missus Warby's a lunatic!' I stumble over to Trevor and grab hold a his hands.

'If he's Edge then I'm white.'

The fat detective tosses a look to his skinny friend and they both smirk at me.

'Sleeping with her, huh Edge?' the fat fella barks.

'Hold on, everybody just hold on.' It's Max's voice.

He stands in the doorway lookin sheepish n red-faced. He looks gobsmacked to see me, then turns to the detectives. 'Sorry boys, wrong man – I've had him checked.'

'I done told ya that! Ya bastards keep ya fucken hands to ya self! The boy ain't no dealer!' I shout it out for all it's worth n haul Trevor to his feet. 'This boy here been a good person in me home n I won't have nobody treatin him like dirt. Yeah, that's right, Max! Leave him alone!' I glass me eyeballs at him.

Max just nods his head. Looking shamed n shufflin his feet, he signals for us to follow him out the door.

The detectives stride out in front a us laughin n makin fuck motions whit their hands. *Fucken pigs. That's all they good for, beltin kids.*

'Oink, oink,' I whisper nudgin Trevor in the ribs.

'Sorry, Mavis,' Max apologises. 'Just a bloody big slip-up.' He turns to Trevor. 'Sorry mate, it's just that you look a lot like this bloke and he's supposed to be in this area somewhere.'

He gives us a weak grin. 'Tell Nevil I'm counting on him to take out the man of the match.'

'Sure will, Max.' I grip Trevor's arm as we walk out onto the street.

'Close shave, love.' I pat his shakin arm. *Poor kid.*

'I think I've had enough of this town. I can't take any more. It's killing me, just torturing me. And those … those *things* back there punched me in the head. It hurt, Missus Dooley.' Trevor's bottom lip pokes out. *He gonna start bawlin for sure.*

'Never mind, love. Ya lucky ya isn't black, else you'd be crawlin outta there. It's over now. Let it pass, love. They'll soon find some other poor sucker to belt.' I look at his tear-stained face. *He ain't hard. He's jus a boy caught up in Nevil's world, my world n the whole friggin town.*

'Who do ya reckon Isaac Edge is?'

Trevor shrugs.

'I reckon whoever he is, he's one smart bastard. But doncha reckon it's all a bit strange how this stuff all seems to be happenin at once?'

'Maybe it's because I'm new here. An easy target.'

'Hmm, I dunno, Trev. I got a gut feelin bout all this. And if I'm right this won't be the end a it.'

A woman can feel it in her bones.

12

Will It Ever End?

Gracie picks at her teeth with a matchstick as she gives Nevil the spitty eye.

'Feminine side, eh. Now what's that sposed to mean?' She directs the question to Trevor.

Trevor throws me a quick look then says, 'Well, it's um, sort of like this – men, well, men have a female side. It's like we have portions of Adam *and* Eve inside of us.' He grins.

She looks at him, her face set in a frown, jaw hangin open. She blinks once, twice, then stares hard at Nevil. 'That'd mean I gotta man inside a me? That I'm really a man?'

'No, I mean, well, yeah, something like that,' Trevor answers, rubbin his stubbly chin. 'It's a subconscious process that has to be developed. It has to be nurtured, like something that has to be encouraged to come out.'

'Come out? Like when you a poofter n you tell the world?' She glares at him, suspicion washin over her face.

'Gracie! That word's not allowed in this house, don't say it!' I bark. *Sayin stuff like that is bound to stick to Nevil.*

'Anyway, it's not like he gonna be like that forever, eh?' I throw a smile at Nevil.

'No, Mum,' he answers, a slight grin on his face.

'Now, what you got to do is keep all this to yourself, Gracie. Nevil n Trevor are workin on somethin portant n if people find out bout this there'll be shit goin down, right.' I narrow me peepers n watch the way she tilts her head to one side, like she can't work me out.

'Yeah, yeah, I know. So how long is this goin on for?' She missiles the question to Nevil, lookin at him like he's a stranger or somethin.

Nevil just looks back at her and shrugs his shoulders.

'Sometimes I wonder, Nevil Dooley, if we were ever meant to be together at all. Seems to me you're spendin all ya time with Trevor, eh. Well, I got dreams too. Ya don't think I'm gonna sit round this shit-hole of a town n wait for ya to be back to normal. Nah, no way. Gracie Marley gonna do somethin with her life.'

'You do what you have to, Gracie. I wouldn't want you to sit around here and wait for me. Yeah, follow your dreams, that's what I reckon.' Nevil offers her a wide smile.

'Goodonya, love, you do what ya have to. But listen, we got this problem whit Max Brown. It'll have to be sorted out otherwise people gonna be runnin me down to the lowest. Trevor, any real ideas to who this Isaac Edge is? I mean, they could pull you in at any ol time, specially the Bullya coppers. Never listen to a cop's promises. It might be okay by Max Brown, but the Bullya boys could be on

157

ya back. Too risky. I don't like the set-up of this whole situation. Somehow it don't seem right,' I say, wonderin how things could go so wrong in this short space a time. But, it only started to go haywire after Trevor turned up on me doorstep. Like he a bad curse or somethin. Like all Mandamooka knowed bout him. Like someone takin piss outta the boy.

'Isaac Edge, who's that?' Gracie asks, turnin round from the fridge.

'Well, love, don't rightly know. Sposed to be some big time drug dealer. Accordin to Max Brown, Isaac Edge is dealin drugs right here in this ol town. Missus Warby n Dotty Reedman told Max that it were Trevor here dealin dope. They seen him walkin through the gate with one of em briefcase things n thought it were full a drugs.'

'Jesus Christ!' Gracie bursts into loud laughter. 'Talk about outta control!'

I reach up into the cupboard, searchin round for a packet a Tim Tams. 'Gracie, ya ever heard anythin bout him?'

'I think Big Boy know who he is.'

'He does?' We all chorus.

'Was talkin bout him there the other day. You know how Big Boy likes his yarndi n shit. Yeah, he reckoned Edge was a real tough fucker. But you know what Big Boy's like, exaggeratin everthin. Yep, he reckoned Edge met him under the ol bridge on the other side a town. He said Edge was from Bullya n he was here to even a score, whatever the fuck that means.' Gracie laughs. 'Reckoned he told him he was after some sheila by the name a Jean Reece. Sounds like Edge real fucked. I mean, ain't no one in Mandamooka called Jean Reece.' She grins.

'Jean Rhys,' I whisper, throwin a wild look at Nevil n Trevor.

Trevor stares at Gracie like she's just thrown a bucket a piss at him, n Nevil, lipsticked-mouth open, eyes bulgin like dog's balls, gapes too.

I feel me gut rumble, the Tim Tams feelin hot n heavy in me sweaty palms as me eyes roam Gracie's face for any signs a bullshit. Me ears start to ring. I walk over n sit down beside her.

'Gracie, ya dead sure bout this?' I ask in me most serious tone a voice.

'That's what Big Boy said. Mum, Nevil, Trevor – what's goin on here?' She looks at each a us.

No one answers. We all just sit starin at her. She wiggles on the chair, blinkin her eyes rapidly, lookin at us like she don't know who we really are.

'It's not my fault! I didn't buy no drugs offa him! Mum, you gotta believe me. Rodge the Dodge gave me some yarndi the other day, that's where I get my stuff from. I didn't buy no drugs offa Edge!' She stands up, her face slack. 'You think I'm some sorta druggie, Mum?' she bursts out, her voice crackin.

'He after Jean?' Nevil whispers, grippin the edge of the table, his knuckles a faint shade of purple.

'But how ... Nah, that can't ...' Trevor begins, then stops, reaches into the fridge and hauls out a beer.

'That can't be right. You musta got your wires crossed, girl,' I say, the sweat poppin out on me dial.

'Nope, that's what he said, "After the bitch Jean." Yep, true words spoken. So are ya Edge?' She half-yells this to Trevor as she walks to the other side a the room.

'No, I ...' Trevor shrinks back into the chair.

'Gracie, when'd this happen?'

'Yesterday, Mum. Why?' She turns to me.

'Did Big Boy see what Edge looks like, eh?'

'I dunno, why don't you ask him yerself. Anyway, what's goin on? Has Nevil done somethin?' She throws him a look a blame.

'No, no, Nevil ain't done nothin. Gracie, you musta heard wrong, cos there ain't no Jean Rhys.' I stop n throw a look at Nevil to test his reaction. He ignores me n goes on starin at Gracie.

Trevor shrugs, his face lined as he fiddles with the beer label.

'Wha? Whatcha mean by that?' Gracie asks, then sits back down.

'There ain't no one here by the name a Jean Rhys. Less you wanna go down to the library n take out a book.' I drum me fingers on the table.

How can a woman explain this, eh? The only Jean Rhys here is in that head a me son's. No such woman, no way, no dice. She don't come any deader n dead.

'Mum, whatcha talkin bout?' Gracie frowns.

'There ain't no woman by the name a Jean Rhys here in Mandamooka. She was a writer, Gracie, a book writer.

Jean's all in Nevil's magination. He woke up one mornin sayin he's her. It's all in his head. Gracie, the woman dead. D-E-D.'

'*Wide Sargasso Sea* and all that,' Trevor puts in, a grin across his pale face.

'About a woman going mad. Antoinette Cosway, married Mister Rochester then he took her to England. She became the woman in the attic. Bertha Rochester in *Jane Eyre*,' Nevil adds.

The room goes quiet. Nobody moves or says a word. Then Gracie twists her lips into a grimace and with one stiff finger points to the top of her head. 'Mad. M-A-D. Nevil, ya lost the fucken plot or what? What the fuck are ya on about!' she explodes.

'Just that there was a Jean Rhys but she's ...' Trevor starts.

'She's me. I'm her,' Nevil replies, slappin a hand to his chest.

'Nevil. Nev, don't ...' I begin.

'You must know *Wide Sargasso Sea* ...?' Trevor smiles.

'Shut up! Shut up!' I shout.

'I'm Jean Rhys!' Nevil yells.

'Nevil! Sit down n shut up!' I smack the table whit me hand.

'Oh Jean, oh Jean,' Nevil sings, his eyes bright and mischievous.

'A very fine writer ...' Trevor takes a sip of beer.

'Jean Rhys, me arse!' I yell at Trevor then glare at Nevil.

'But now, with Jean, the thing was—' Trevor starts.

'Nough! Shut ya traps! Shut up! Just shut the hell up! Nough a this fucken shit!' I shake me fist in front a Nevil, me voice-box stretched to the limit.

Everybody shuts up.

Gracie, by this time, has left her chair and stands near the door, like she gonna tear through it any minute. She chews on her bottom lip n looks at all a us like we all gone in the head. Her face all screwed up like skin on a lemon. She look real suss. Not likin this a bit.

'I … I gotta go,' she mumbles then rushes out the door.

'Gracie, Gracie, love. Stop, you gotta know bout this. Gracie, don't go. It's all a mistake. Gracie, Nevil got head trouble. He's goin crazy mad or somethin. Love, he's sick. A sick boy. We was jokin, yeah a big joke, har, har. Grraacieee!' I puff and pant after her as she tears out the front gate.

'Mavis, yahooo, Mavis.'

I turn to the scratchy voice comin from the other side a the fence. I spin round. 'Missus Warby?' I stride towards the fence line.

'Oh, hello there. Nice day.' She smiles over at me, the eye spotters hangin from her neck.

'That's enough. I've had it! Why the hell did ya tell Max Brown that Trevor's a drug dealer? Tell me that!' I blast her, wantin to tear her ol face right off.

'Well, I never,' she begins with a horrified tone. Then not missin a beat she says, 'Remember, Mavis, say "No" to drugs!'

162

I gawk up at her. *The hide a it. The fucken hide a it! Jeesus Christ Almighty, a woman just can't win no matter what!* 'What are you on bout?' I hiss.

'I know what's going on over there. You can tell me now while he's out of earshot. *I can help you*, Mavis. I was never the one to turn my back on those in need. No, as my late husband, Reginald, would say – "Ivy Warby, you have the biggest and kindest heart a man's ever come across." I can get you out of there, Mavis. With the Lord's help I'll free you from the Devil's arms. I've got weapons in my house. A gun,' she whispers, one eye turned towards me front door.

'Missus Warby, ya got a gun in there! Don't you go pullin it on anybody! Anyway, it's all a mistake. Trevor ain't no drug dealer. Trevor is definitely not Isaac Edge!' I blurt out, me head thuddin. *She one twisted ol sheila.*

'Oh my God!' she gasps, her eyes wide, one hand placed near her heart. 'Nevil, what has he done to Nevil!'

'Nuthin. Missus Warby, you gotta stop all this! It's makin me life hell! Ain't no drugs, no nuthin! Hear that! Nuthin!' I bust me guts.

Her mouth opens and she utters a little, 'Oh.'

'That's right, you ol stickybeak! Ya makin Mavis Dooley's life a livin hell! You n that Reedman bitch!' I shake a fist at her.

Not put off she says, 'Well, I know you're in denial, Mavis. But, Ivy Warby can get you out of that hell hole! Seen some mighty things in my life, had to deal with some real bastards, and there's nothing, nothing that will stop me from helping those in need.

'Mavis, I will be your rock. God will guide me to help you through this terrible time in your life. Yes, he will.' She reaches out for me hand. 'It's all right, love. I know how scared you are. Threats usually do that to a person,' she says, her eyes feverishly bright.

I fall back from her not believin me ears. *She can't be tole. Ain't no language in this world is gonna make her listen. She thinks Trevor's threatnin me. Oh Jeesus!*

'Jus forget it. Don't worry bout it,' I reply in a strained and weary voice. As I turn away there's a shout. 'Stop! Stop right there where you are!'

Max Brown stands at the gate, hat in one hand, the other resting on the revolver at his side. 'Mavis Dooley, I'm here in an official capacity. I'm here to take you and Nevil in.' He walks towards me, a sorry look on his face.

'Why?' I whisper, me legs weak, me heart thumpin slow.

'Drugs. Now, no trouble, Mavis. Just doing my job is all.' He grips me arm tight, as he steers me through the kitchen doorway. Nevil brings his head up from the table eyeshada n lipstick smudged cross his dial. Trevor looks at me, then at Max.

'Oh no, not again,' he croaks.

'On your feet, Nevil!' Max barks. 'I'm taking you in, son.'

'What now? No, no, don't tell me, I already know. Drugs, right? Yeah, what else would it be.' Nevil shakes his head wearily then gets up slowly to his feet. He glances at Max with a sour look, and comes over to where I'm standin. He loops a strong arm into mine and together we go out. I look across to the curb and parked there is the gleamin gungie machine, crouchin on the bitumen like the car from hell.

'Get in, son.' Max opens the door. 'Mavis, you can sit in the front with me.'

I look up to see the neighbours comin out of their houses. Some of em point at the car, their mouths flipped open, their eyes wide. Others crowd round Missus Warby like a gaggle a old ducks, as she stands pointin a bony finger at Trevor, who is inchin his way back into the house. Missus Warby leads em forward, they close in on him. A small shiver dimples me arms as we speed off down the street.

13

The Set-up

The fat D screws up his piggy eyes and stares at both of us. His skinny friend stands in the corner, arms crossed, lips curled back in a snarl. At the far end of the table, Max Brown sits lookin real nervy. He can't stop lookin at Nevil's lips. *Like he be sussin it's lipstick but not too sure.*

'So, what's your story?' Fat Man looks at me then Nevil.

I shrug me shoulders. I don't know. Nevil throws me a look n jus grins.

'We have received a number of phone calls naming you and that son of yours.' Skinny suit stands behind me. 'We know you've had contact with her, Missus Dooley.'

'We mean Edge's courier, of course you know that.' Fat Man glares at me.

I smile up at him, all innocent. 'I dunno. Anyway, who the hell ya talkin bout?' I ask, pickin small pieces a fluff off me skirt. *Me gut tells me who he's talkin bout. Yep, it's come to this. A woman just sick to death of it all.*

I know who he's gonna say. There ain't a thing I can tell em. Nuh, ain't jackshit ol Mavis Dooley can say.

'Might make it easier on yourself if you just tell them the truth, Mavis,' Max says, raising his thick eyebrows at me.

'It's all just another mistake. For God's sake! I don't know who ya askin bout! A woman ain't no mind reader! First ya haul Trevor in, sayin he's the Edge, next you got me n Nevie in sayin we know all bout it.

'Max, it's no good for the boy's nerves, all this business. You know he got the big game comin up. Can't take it, can you, son? Max, you know what we're like. A woman ain't got nuthin to do whit all this. Nev don't even touch the shit, no good for his trainin. Nah, Max, I thought you knew us.' I shake my head with all the disgust I can muster up.

Max Brown looks at me with a flicker of apology. 'Sorry, Mavis, but when we get a lead we have to follow it,' he says, in a soft tone a voice.

'It's gonna wear the boy down. The Rammers'll take this year's match out. Yep, n all Mandamooka gonna know who made Nevil a bag a nerves. They'll lose the big match, you jus watch.' I tighten me lips. *A woman jus gettin tired a this shit.*

'Look, just tell us who she is and I'll let you both go,' Max says, his face goin pink.

Ol Max is all right really. A woman can't blame the man for doin his job. But I gotta be careful whit what I say to him. He might spread it round town.

'I done tole you I don't know. Maybe, if ya tell me who we talkin bout here a woman can get some sorta idea.' I chew me bottom lip.

167

'Nevil, come on, boy, tell them who it is,' Max urges.

'Um … I—' Nevil stops abruptly, just as a voice from the doorway yells out, 'What the hell?'

I swing round on my chair and smile with relief as Booty strides in the room.

'Max! What the hell is me sister and nephew doin here!' he booms, his face steely, eyes slitted.

Max pauses for a fraction of a second. 'We got a lead.'

'Well, there ain't no lead here whit them.' Booty glares at the Ds. His chest is puffed right out in front a him, his arms swingin back n forth.

'Get this man out of here!' Skinny D orders Max.

'What you got them in for?' Booty turns to Max.

'Drugs. Saying we're in a rackateering business,' Nevil pipes up, wipin the back a his hand cross his lipsticked mouth.

Booty's gob flips open. He looks at each of us then bursts into loud gut laughter. 'Drugs! Drugs!' he splutters, one hand holdin his big gut as he gasps for air.

'Yeah, sayin we know who this courier person is,' I put in, smirking at Fat Man. *See, Fatty, ya got the wrong fellas again. Fatty n Skinny – good cop, bad cop, har, har, haaaaaarrr. That's a hoot.*

'You fellas got the wrong people, that's a fact.' Booty laughs, as Max leads him out the door.

'Who is this woman?' Skinny pulls out a chair and sits in front a me while Fatty stands in front a Nevil and gives him a don't-fuck-with-me look.

'Anytime, son,' Fatty says. 'Tell me and you can go home. There's no use of protecting her.'

'Now, Missus Dooley, I'd reckon you're a decent woman and have your problems but this courier will take you down with her when we bring her in. She'll say it was you. One name. Just one name. That's all I want.'

'Mister, I swear to God I dunno. If I did I'd *definitely tell ya*!'

'Okay, time for hardball. Who is Jean Rhys?' He grins. Gotcha!

'Whaa?' I look at him, me chin droppin to me chest.

'That's right, Missus Dooley, Jean Rhys – R-H-Y-S.'

I sit right back in the chair, me ol head spinnin like a bottle top. Skinny grins at me like he's onto something. Like he said the magic word. *What can I tell the man? Anythin a woman says gonna sound friggin womba. Tell him Jean Rhys a writer n that she carked it a long time ago? Tell him me Nev thinks he's Jean Rhys? What does a woman say? Yep, gonna sound like I'm the one fulla drugs, eh.*

So I say, 'Go to the library. You want your woman, go down to Lizzie there at the library.' I tighten me mouth. *I've had nough a Jean Rhys. Sick, sick to death of hearin that bloody name.*

'Lizzie at the library is Jean Rhys?' Skinny cocks an eyebrow, a triumphant smile on his face.

'No, no, not Lizzie! Just go n ask her bout this friggin Jean Rhys!'

Just then, across the room, the fat D bursts into laughter, his face scrunched up n red as he points at Nevil.

169

'Fucking maniac,' he gasps, holding onto the edge of the table like it'll keep him standing up. 'Reckons *he's* Jean!'

Skinny casts a glance at Nevil and offers a weak smile. Yep, one kid fucked from the drugs, his look seems to suggest.

Next thing Max comes back and whispers something into the fat man's ear. Then he turns to me. 'Righto, Mavis, you're free to go.' He offers a hand to help me to my feet.

'I want Nevil to come whit me.' I stand, hands on hips n glare at all a them. *Youse ain't gonna mess whit me boy's head, no way. Ain't gonna rip into him like youse did to poor ol Trevor. No, no.*

'On your feet, boy.' The fat cop slaps Nevil cross the back.

'Hey, no need to hit so hard! Anyway, you'll never find Jean. Hear that, *never*,' Nevil says with a smirk, smudged lips curled into an oily grin.

'Oh, we'll find her and when we do we are gonna haul your arse in here, boy! By the way, Sonny, what's that shit on your lips?' The fat cop peers hard at Nevil's mouth. 'Fuck me flying! The boy's a fucking fag!' He takes a step back, a pretend look a disbelief on his face.

'It's not lipstick! It's special stuff Doctor Chin gave him for his sore lips! Don't call my son a fag, FAT BOY!' I yell at him, me dander right up n deadly. *Callin me son a queen.*

'Settle down, little woman,' Skinny D says, backin up his partner.

170

LITTLE WOMAN! Who the fuck he think he is?

'Listen here, you skinny arse creep, don't call me LITTLE WOMAN! Jus who are you, eh, eh!' I move towards him, seein fucken red. I anger up mad. *I'm gonna get that little goona boy!* I throw one hand at him and shove him so hard he stumbles back and falls on the table.

'Leave us alone!' I shout, as Max and Fat Cop grab my arms and pin them to me sides.

'Mum, Mum, leave it alone. Come on, Mum, leave it out,' Nevil pleads, fear across his face.

'Get her out of here!' The fat D bellows at Max.

As I cut it towards the door I can't help but leave em somethin to think about. I say, 'Wait till you ol boys get a load a Jean Rhys!' Then I laugh – really, really laugh, til me gut cramps up n me bladder threatens to burst. *That'll twist em. Huh, fuckery.*

Max leads me to the front desk. He motions for me to sit down then turns to Nevil and says, 'I think you should hear this too.'

As I settle in I hear a noise from behind me and turn round.

'It's all right, Sis.' Booty grins, his arms crossed, his eyes glued on Max.

'Look, Mavis, this whole business is getting out of control here. Now, if you do know anything, anything at all – this goes for you too, Nevil – please for God's sake tell me! I'm the one looking like a damned fool. What am I supposed to do when I receive these calls telling me that you and Nevil here are involved?

'Hang on, now, hang on before you go off the handle, I think that someone out there is trying to set you or young Nevil up. I don't know why but I've the feeling there's other forces at work here. A big hunch, actually. Any ideas?' Max looks from me to Nev and back again.

'But why … I mean, who?' I stare at Max. *A set-up?*

'Who made the phone calls? I mean, we haven't got any enemies, have we, Ma?' Nevil throws the last question at me. By this time he's wiped all the lipstick off whit the back a his hand.

'Well, love, I don't really know.' I think a everybody I know who'd do somethin like this. I come up empty. *Who'd be low nough, is the question?*

Max sighs. 'Therein is the mystery. The first call was from a woman calling herself Davida Dalrymple, the second from a man calling himself John Holmes. Obviously fake names but I can tell you this – those calls were all made here in Mandamooka. Someone out there is setting you up for this Edge business. Someone has a real problem with both or one of you. Done anything to anyone lately?'

'No, absolutely not. Who'd wanna waste they time settin *us* up? And why'd you bring us in?' I study Max's face.

He turns round and throws a quick glance towards the door. Hunching his shoulders forward, Max leans over the counter and whispers, 'Got to make it look good in front of the boys. – Like they told you, they received the same calls in Bullya. As you know, it's my duty to follow these things up.'

'So, these callers told you that it was me and Mum?' Nevil frowns.

'Yes, said you both knew where Jean was. Matter of fact, said you had her at the house there. See, it's like this. Jean is supposed to be Edge's courier pigeon and apparently she's here in Mandamooka hiding out. That's what the story is so far.'

'Max, there's no person in this town called Jean Rhys.' I lean closer to his face. 'Max, the woman don't exist. She's some dead writer. That's right, there was a Jean Rhys a long time ago but she jus don't exist any more. No such person here in Mandamooka.'

'She's a woman all in Nevil's head.' Booty steps closer, too.

'What d'you mean?' Max frowns as though we're takin the piss.

'Jus that. He made her all up. Like a big trick on everybody. Yeah, a big joke. You know how young fellas like to arse about. Nothin else in this town for them to do. Tell him bout the *big joke*, Nevil.'

Nevil casts me a dangerously pissed-off look then says, 'I'm Jean. I'm the real Jean Rhys.' *Take that.*

'Shut up, Sonny Jim!' Booty slaps him cross the shoulder blades. 'The boy's losin his mables. Those Ds got him screwed up here.' Booty points to his skull.

'Was always the one for bad nerves, me Nevil. Don't listen to that rot, Max. He ain't been hisself lately.

173

All this drug business wearin us thin. I jus can't take this any more! Me blood pressure's been playin up n everythin. I not a well woman, Max.' I slump forward, me hand cross me forehead. *Reckon I must look real down like. Can't have Max askin too many questions.*

Booty, knowin the real deal, sighs deep. 'It's all right, Sis, Max here knows what you like. Hard life n all. Any other woman wouldn't a took it like you. Bringin up the boy by yerself n strugglin, yeah, bloody fine job you did. That's me sister for ya, Max, a battler. Tryin her little heart out to bring the boy up real decent like.' Booty scratches his fat gut, a crooked grin on his sweat n drenched face.

'Don't cry, Mavis. I know what sort of person you are. I was never convinced that any of this had anything to do with you. I remember when young Nevil here used to play in the school football team, had a lot of talent back then. As I have always said, there's a boy that'll go far in life. Mavis, I don't want you to blame me for any of this. I want you to know that I have to do all this otherwise those Bullya blokes will be on my back.' He looks me in the eye, a sorry look on his dial.

Booty pats me shoulder. 'Those Ds got no right to talk to her and Nevil the way they done. My sister and nephew ain't no drug dealers, Max.'

'Well, let's just hope this will all be sorted out soon. I would advise you to keep on your toes. There's someone out there that's got a dangerous grudge against both of you.'

I stand to my feet n wipe away the crocodile tears. 'Thanks, Max,' I sniff. Grabbin Nevil tight by the arm. I steer him full force out the door.

When we're on the street again Booty explodes: 'Fucken Jean Rhys! What are you, a fucken loony tunes, Sonny Jim! Goin in there like that! A man oughta kick that black arse a yours! Can't ya see whatcha doin to ya poor ol mother!' Booty hits Nevil cross the back a the head. 'Fucken wake up to yourself otherwise I'm gonna have to do somethin bout all this shit! Nevil, ya not a bloody woman n that's that! If God meant for ya to have a woman thing between ya legs then that's what he'd a given ya!' Booty's eyes are bulgin outta his head.

I ignore his shouts as he drags Nevil down the road. Me thoughts are on who's settin us up n for what.

Dotty Reedman, would she have the guts? Hmm, yeah, cos the woman done hate me, she do. Maybe she wanna be gettin rid a me so as she can have Terry to herself. Yep, can jus see her dial – happy as a pig in shit if she can do me over for Terry. Then again, maybe it's cos Nevil busted her son up. Yeah, he smashed Jerry. Gave the boy a hidin.

Missus Warby – who'd really know what goes on in that one's head. She a madwoman for sure. Would she do this to us? Yeah, she would, thinkin she doin God's work n everythin. Doin a good deed.

Darryl Kane? Maybe, since I busted him in front a the bar. He promised revenge like, too. Don't reckon he'd forget a woman doin him over like that. Causin him shame in front a his big hero pals.

Terry Thompson – dunno, doubt it. I mean, what would he have to gain by doin this to us? Nah, wouldn't be Terry. Anyway, I hope it ain't cos I'd be real disappointed if it was. Hmm, come to think a it, a person don't really know a lot bout the man. Sure, he nice n everythin but he could be a shyer. Shyin behind a mask. Jus like Nevil. Cept Nevil don't hide it.

Anybody's a suspect really. I do know one thing – it can't be Jean Rhys! She's dead. Ain't no dead woman come back n lived in a man, that much a woman do know. Then again, it's a funny world, strange things happen ta people all the time. Yeah, they sure do when I think bout it.

Anythin likely to happen. Jus don't be hangin on that call, bingo, ol girl, cos things are changin round here all the time.

Ya don't have a chance in hell if ya not on ya ol warty toes.

14

Isaac Edge

Terry Thompson gangles near the doorway, holdin a garden fork and lookin in at the room. He watches everyone closely. I watch him closely. *The man look myall standin there like that.* Trousers caked whit dirt n his shirt-sleeves torn n fallin down his skinny arms. His face got that worn-out look bout it. Like the man can't get nough sleep. He's lookin for someone. Dotty Reedman? Thinkin a her I turn in me chair and scan the room. There she sits at the far end of the table.

Big dirty gold hair scraped up into a bun-like turnout. Lips painted up fire-engine red. Eyelids a washed out blue whit black rimmed edges. Pink shit stainin her cheekbones. Long fingernails, purple, bruise-purple.

The woman look like one of em hookers. Sellin they bodies for a bit a coin. How much, Dotty, for a roll in the hay? Har, de har. She must have some sorta psycho hmmm, is that the word they use? Like when people know whatcha thinkin bout. Yeah, psycho power. Cos she turn real fast like n eyeball at me cross the room. Snake eyes screwed n scrunched up, small n spite-green. She sticks her tongue out at me – like the woman's a little snot-nosed kid. Yeah, wanna play rough, Potty Dotty. I give her a big, bright smile, then when I'm sure no one lookin I flip me hand n give her the middle finger – *take that, you horse-faced bitch!*

She reels back in her chair like I done hit her or somethin. Then she looks over at Terry in the doorway, gives him a wave n runs her tongue cross her lips. *I know what she doin. Yeah, n Terry bein Terry, he'll be sucked right in – go on, Terry, that big hair will getcha! She'll catch ya up in it! Like a fly in a spider web.*

Is she the one who set me n Nev up for that Isaac Edge business? Wouldn't put it past her. Be jus her type a jig. The woman hate us, she do. Maybe I'll go cross there n knock the piss right outta that friggin skinny body a hers. She a bad egg – half-boiled, runny, full a poison yolk.

I turn me attention away from her and look at Terry. He spots me then gives a little wave. 'Hey, Mave,' he mouths.

Me gut flips all bout the place – fish in a barrel. Me mouth all dried out like. I wonder what I look like to him. *Hope I look sexy! Hey, lookout! Can a woman be sayin em things bout herself? SEXY. Sexy Mavis? Arrhhh, don't be thinkin shit, woman. You ain't sexy like that piece a meat cross there. But all a same I look all right, I do. The dress I got on is new – Nevil n Trevor got it for me. Bright, covered in flower patterns, all colours, the hem almost up on me knee! An a real funky – hey is that the word – drop-down neckline, part of me chest showin – nah, just peekin up. Before I left home, Nev put some shit on me face; lipstick, eyeshada stuff, n done me hair up in a braid. I reckon I must look all right cos Trevor was real pressed! An, he's a man; well, I think he is. Yeah, could look good. I feelin solid n all.*

Hey, lookout there! Here comes Gwenny Hinch! She look charged or somethin. Eyes red n puffed out.

'Mavis, how are ya?' She pulls out a chair to sit down beside me.

'Takin up bingo now?' I ask, tryin to sniff the air round her. Tryin to see if she charged.

'As if!' she snorts. 'I had to come here and see you. I got real problems, Mave.' She fidgets with her hands.

'*Five!* A high five! Anyone got a five?' Hettie yells out.

'Like what?'

'*Seven!* A sinful seven! That's it girls, seven!'

'Um, don't you go slammin a woman but—' Gwenny pauses, drops her head and stares at her hands.

'*Two.* Yes that's right, two! Good old number two!'

'Darryl?' I suss out. 'Somethin to do whit Darryl Kane. That's it, hey?'

'*Fifty-four.* Fifty-four, Terry at the door. Fifty-four, anyone have a fifty-four!'

'Sorta. I – um. You gonna go right off what I gotta say.'

'*Eight.* Eight, don't be late. Girls, anyone for an eight!'

'Shittin hell, Gwen get to the bloody point!' I watch her eyes slide round the room. The woman don't wanna look at me. She knowed I be sussin on her.

'*Three.* Three. That number three!' Hettie shouts.

'I'm seein him again,' she whispers, offerin me a shamejob look.

179

'*Ten*, ten, ten. He's at it again! Anyone for a ten!'

'Oh no, don't tell me, it's Darryl Kane, ain't it? You seein that piece a shit, again!' I look at her like she's gone mad. *Maybe she has. Finally lost the plot.*

'I can't help it. I love him, Mavis. He's leaving Samantha. He promised me that. He did. Mavis, he's tellin the truth, I just know.'

Hettie yells loud and clear cross the room, 'Who's got the bingo today? Come on, ladies, one of you out there must have all the right numbers. Three hundred bucks is the jackpot. Come on, who's the lucky person?'

'You mad you is. After what he done to ya! Gwenny, what's up whit ya, woman? He's a friggin arsehole! Yeah, go on then, let him go round spruikin more shit bout how good black women is in the sack! He was gonna put the boot into ya there at the pub. Ya forgot that mighty fast like.' I glare at her, teeth grindin, me nostrils flarin.

'Don't be shy. There's some lucky woman out here today. Come on, step up whoever you are,' Hettie yells, circlin the room like a vulture.

'He's changed, he has. Even got a new job in Bullya. Bought himself a flash car and the old Hunter house by the river there. He said he's sorry for everythin.'

'Come on, now. *Someone* must have the *numbers*!'

'All bulldust! He a woman-bashin creep. Ya jus sucked right in, like that ol Terry over there. Yep, it's all jus some sorta mad game to some peoples.' I glare round the room.

'You my best friend, Mavis. I – well, Big Boy don't

know jus yet, but I gotta tell him. I thought, well—' She stops and eyeballs me.

'Any numbers, Mavis?' Hettie stops at the table, a hopeful smile on her face.

'Hey, Hettie. Here's my card, can you check it please?' I hand it to her and watch as she strides cross the room. *Person wouldn't be lucky nough to win it again.*

'Yeah, Gwen, what?' I turn back to her.

'I thought maybe you or Nev could like say somethin to him,' she pleads.

'To Big Boy! Geez, somethin terrible wrong when ya can't tell ya own son bout things. I'm not sayin nuthin, Gwen. Nah, that your job.'

'Mavis, Mavis!' Hettie yells, as she races cross the floor. 'You won! You won the bingo! Three hundred big bucks!' She laughs as she hands back me card.

'I did? Well, talk bout luck, eh? Thanks, Hettie.' *I won. I won. How lucky can one woman be. Yippeee! Take that, Dotty!*

'Goodonya! You the luckiest person I know.' Gwen pats me on the back. 'Anyway, now listen, Mave, I gotta ask you somethin really important. You ever heard of a woman called Jean that lives round here somewhere?'

'Jean? Whatcha talkin bout?' I do a double-take n stare at her.

'Heard Darryl the other day talkin bout this woman called Jean. She seems to work for him or somethin. I know somethin's goin down and it's gotta lot to do whit Jean. Maybe he's screwin her too, eh.'

'Don't tell me it's Jean Rhys! Is that her name? Jean Rhys?' I gape, me mouth unhinged. *It comes full circle. Back to bite me. Jean'll never leave a woman alone. Yep, it never gonna end fer me. I can see that now. Since the day me boy woked up whit that mad idea it's been nuthin but trouble whit all this business.*

'Hey, yeah that's it. Jean Rhys, that's her name!' Gwen blurts out, eyes wide.

'Works for Darryl Kane? She works for Darryl?' Me eyes bulge. 'You mustta heard wrong, Gwen.' *Like a nightmare.*

'Nope, Jean Rhys, that's who he was talkin bout. Reckoned it were all a big joke. Heard him tellin some fella from Bullya what a real hard worker Jean is. Yep, even reckoned she were gonna do some dirty work for him. Whatcha make a that, eh?' She looks at me with question marks in her eyes.

Me gut drops. I grip the edge a the table, me knuckles throbbin. Blood pressure risin fast. I feel giddy. 'Jean Rhys don't exist!' I yell it out. 'What the hell's wrong whit people in this town! Jean Rhys is a figure of magination in Nevil's head! She's not even alive! The woman dead! She a dead woman!' I turn away from Gwen n look round the room. *It be the death a me fer sure.*

The room goes dead quiet. Everyone stares back; Hettie's frozen to the spot in the middle a the room; Terry, mouth open, looks at me like I a loony; Dotty smirkin n smilin n all the others nudgin each other n lookin at me like I done pulled down me bloomers n

182

pissed on the floor in front a em. *This time I done it good n proper. Yep, now the whole town knows. Well, that jus tough shit, ain't it, Mavis big-trap Dooley. Ya always knew the day'd come when all this would blow up. Yep, all cos a some dead writer. Finished right up.*

'Gee, Mave, no need to scream about it,' Gwen says, then coughs shame like into her hand.

'Gwen, I reckon *Darryl Kane is Isaac Edge*. Listen, Max Brown come over n hauled all our arses off to the pig shop. He reckons me boy's best mate, Trevor, is Isaac Edge – the one dealin drugs to everybody. See, Max reckoned somebody had it in for me n Nev, too.' Me voice drops, 'Darryl, that's who.'

Gwen stares back at me, blinks, turns from me and stares at the doorway. After about a second or two she turns back and says, 'What the fuck you on about? Mavis, ya been hittin the piss or somethin? Ya not yourself any more. Is this ya way of gettin me away from Darryl? I know ya hate his guts, Mave, yeah. But I'm not gonna be listenin to this stuff if that's what ya tryin to do to me.'

'Jesus Christ! Gwen, it ain't any a that! It's bout Jean Rhys! Jean Rhys, Isaac Edge n this shit that's been goin on. I can't tell you everythin now but jus come home whit me n I'll explain it all. It's a long story. Trust me, ya'll know what I been goin through all this time. Ain't been easy.' I get to me feet feelin like a sack a shit.

'Well then, it better be good, Mavis. I'm sick a people tellin me all sorts a shit. I jus dunno who to believe any more. Seems like even you changed somewhere long the line. Like ya ain't Mavis Dooley no more.'

'Ya believe me, Gwenny, I wouldn't lie. Anyhow, whatcha mean I ain't Mavis Dooley any more?' I turn n face her.

'Jus that ya seem different somehow. Like ya been changin into somebody else. Sorta like ya hidin somethin. Oh, I dunno, sorry Mave, maybe I'm grog-fucked or somethin.' She looks at me, sussin eyes crawlin over me dial.

'Talkin shit, woman. I ain't different.' I throw an arm round her shoulder as we head for the door.

Terry blocks the doorway. 'How are ya, love?' he asks, in a syrupy voice, all con job.

'All right. Get outta my way.' I push past him n step outside. No time for any shit today. A woman got serious business to tend to. *Drug business.*

'Hey, you looken good. Can I come over and see you later?' he calls out, all smooth.

'Yeah, whatever,' I reply, a flutter in me guts. *But, eh, ol girl, maybe Terry's in on this Edge stuff. Go on big notin yaself. Who really knows what goes on in that head a his? Ya don't really know a lot bout the man. Could be a killer for all ya know. Watch ya steps there, ya might go arse-over. Terry could be sussin on ya.*

As me and Gwen go down the steps, Dotty flies past, looks over her shoulder and gives me a nasty grin. 'Cheat. Bingo cheat! Bitch! I'm going to get you, Dooley! It's only a matter of time,' she says in a cracked, I-really-hate-you voice. I watch as she hurries to her car. Before she gets in she casts me one more look, dangerous and hateful. I smile at her. *See, ya don't worry me one little bit.*

'Fuck ya. Gorn ya ugly slut!' Gwen shouts, wavin a fist in her direction.

Wish Dotty'd leave a person lone n get some sorta life steada pickin me to death. Gee, one a these days I'm gonna really bust me guts – then she'll be sorry. She's in this Edge shit fer sure. I'd bet me life on it.

We motor on towards my place. I wonder how I'll tell Gwen everythin. A woman gotta tell her the whole story. It ain't gonna be pretty.

I push the front door open and we go inside. The house is too quiet. *Where Nevil n Trevor at?* I step into the kitchen. Shock knocks me back into the wall. I grab hold a me throat. I struggle to breathe.

Everything looks hazy. Me legs are burnin up like a red-hot iron branded on me. I be stamped for a turn – I slippin fast. *Why did Jean ever come into me life? She killin me. A dead woman killin me. I dying.*

Sitting at the table drinkin tea n eating biscuits is Missus Warby and Big Boy. At the other end a the table sits Nevil, frocked n made up like a paintin. This ain't no joke. Big Boy n Missus Warby would have to suss that.

Spots appear before me eyes. I throw out an arm towards Gwen. I must be dreamin. It's a dream, magination. Too much stress for a woman. Doctor Chin, gotta see him. I fight for air. *A woman dead.*

15

He's Crossed That River

'Nevil … Nevil, what the fuck is on your face?' Gwen asks, her eyeballs poppin outta her skull as she walks towards him.

'Yeah, well, hello to you too. It's make-up. You know, lipstick and eyeshadow,' Nevil says, smilin up at her.

'It's an experiment,' Trevor interrupts, castin me small glances as I prop meself gainst the wall. *Phew, saved by Trevor!*

Gwen shakes her head. 'Huh, funny, very funny. You n your jokes, Nevil Dooley.' Then she turns to Big Boy. 'Anyway, what're you doin here, Boy?'

'Come to get the Nev for trainin,' he replies, shruggin his shoulders. 'What, a grown man can't go nowhere less he ask his mother?'

'Missus Warby, whatcha doin here?' I ask, me mouth dry.

'I brought some shortbread over for Nev, I know how much he likes it,' she answers, tappin the side a the tin teacup.

'Well, since you're here I might as well ask you some questions bout this drugs business. That is if you know anythin, which a woman thinks ya might.' I show me teeth, pull out a chair n plonk down beside her. The woman got the grace to look shamejob face. *Now fer some grillin.*

'What drug business, Missus D?' Big Boy butts in, reachin down to haul a beer from the half-opened carton on the floor.

'Well, Boy, somebody's been phonin Max n em other cops at Bullya there n tellin em we drug pigeons, me n Nevie. Seems somebody's got a hate gainst us. Hhmm, now I wonder who'd do that?' I turn round quick n raise my eyebrows at Missus Warby.

'Oh no, you don't, Mavis. I had nothing to do with it all. If you want to accuse anyone you can blame Dorothy Reedman for that. I just—' Missus Warby pauses, gatherin her defences like, then her eyes flash. 'Yes, she's the one that told me. What could I do? Mavis, I thought you were in trouble here! But now I know the real story.' She stops, then wipes at her eyes.

I scan the woman's dial. *Is she really that cracked? Yep, I reckon she is.* 'Look Missus Warby, what ya done was stupid. Yeah, bloody stupid! Now, I know ya lookin out for me n Nev but this shit has gotta stop!' I watch the way her hands fiddle whit the tablecloth. I push on. 'Right. Now did Dotty mention the name Jean Rhys or Isaac Edge? Jus think. Cos it's real portant.'

'Hey, I know those names!' Big Boy bursts out.

'Yeah, from where?' Gwen sits beside him, her eyes takin in his face.

'I er … I – um. Don't worry bout it. Let's jus say I seen Edge the other day down at the old bridge n he said somethin bout this Jean.' He coughs n puts a hand over his mouth, as if he can't say any more.

'What he look like? Paint us a picture, Boy.' I scope in on him. *Come on, Boy. Drop ya guts, son. Let it all out.*

'Weeelll, see, the problem is, the fella was standin *right under the bridge.* Had a hat on so I couldn't really get a good go at him. Said somethin bout Jean bringin in some good shit from Bullya.' He laughs n takes a swig a beer.

'Yes, that's right! Dotty mentioned those names!' Missus Warby all but screams out in her excitement. 'Seems Max told her to keep a good eye on Jerry, her son, because some people were targeting all the young folk in Mandamooka! Drugs, that's it, drugs!'

'Gwen, this drug dealer Isaac Edge has got to be Darryl Kane; Jean Rhys don't come into it. I reckon somebody got they wires crossed on that one, though I don't know how.' I puzzle it out. *Someone got the wrong message it seems. We're accidents, I reckon. Yep, me n Trev n Nev jus bystanders. Don't reckon Jean got a lot to do whit this – or do she?*

'But Dotty knew about it, didn't she!' Missus Warby pipes up.

'That's right. How did she find out?' I suss in on her.

'Well, I've got a small confession to make.' Missus Warby stops and clears her throat. She begins slow, head down, 'Dotty came over to my place one day and she got on my spot by the fence there and looked over. Apparently – this is what she told me – Trevor there was talking into one of them fancy phones, you know, the ones you can walk around with.'

'A mobile,' Gwen interrupts.

'Yes, thanks, one of them. She said Trevor was telling someone at the other end about this woman staying here. He mentioned her name – Jean Rhys. And that this Jean woman was fooling everyone and that when all the town knew the real truth, the shi … the truth would knock them all out. He said she was a genius, this woman Jean.' Missus Warby stops and sighs wearily. Like it's all too much for her to take in.

'Trust Dotty to get it all ballsed up. Only Dotty could take somethin like that n blow it all up.' I nod me head tiredly.

'Who is Jean Rhys?' Gwen, Big Boy and Missus Warby chorus.

'Don't ask me. Ask Trevor n Nev there.' I point at both of them, an angry glare on me dial.

Trevor coughs loudly, clears his throat, then looks to Nevil. 'Will I?'

'Go right ahead.' Nevil shrugs with a sigh, then goes quiet, his eyes tight shut.

'Jean was someone we just sort of made up for this experiment. Now, I can't tell you everything but I can tell you it's all got out of control. I came here to try and help a good friend of mine. Now it seems that this whole town has taken something I said and misinterpreted it. There's no Jean Rhys that's a drug pigeon, a courier. Someone must have said her name to someone else, and

Mandamooka being the town it is – just ran with the entire thing.'

'Added,' I jump in. 'Built more on more: Sorta links in a chain, whit me n Nev bein the weak link on the arse enda it. Weighin it down till it weaken. Talk, right outta control. People takin lies for fact!'

'Exactly. Jean Rhys was a famous writer. She is not someone who's actually *alive*. To make it a little bit easier for all of you, I should tell you about myself ...' Trevor stops midway and looks over to the doorway.

'Trev, how the fuck are ya!' Booty strides in from work, covered from head to toe in blood. *The man a walkin abattoir.*

'Yeah, it's Darryl! It's got to be Darryl,' Gwen yells, the truth written cross her face. 'Mavis, remember the night you decked him down at the pub there! Remember, n he swore he was gonna getcha for makin him look a right jerk in fronta everyone!'

'That's it! He *said* he was gonna get me, eh. The friggin bastard!'

'Mum, what are you on about?'

'I dropped him cos he was tryin to kick Gwen in the guts. The whole bar was gawkin n laughin at him. Nah, he didn't like that. Shamed him up good n proper a woman did.'

'Why, Mum? What's goin down?' Big Boy throws a look a suspicion at Gwen.

'He was having an affair whit your Mumma! The bastard was goin round town tellin em all bout how good

190

'No way! This is right out of my league,' Trevor replies.

Yep, the boy learnin all bout Booty. Probably shittin hisself in case he gotta fight somebody. A woman don't blame him for that. The boy been to hell n back since he done turned up here in this town.

I look at Booty watchin Nevil, weighin him up like a chook in a raffle. *N the raffle bout to be drawn – who the winner? Oh yeah, Mister Darryl Kane. Take home ya prize, Mr Kane. Throw that ol baldy piece a meat in ya oven – roast him good now. Then serve him up whit spuds n punkin; slap some gravy on that ol leg. Eat it, then shit it out. Good tucker, eh.*

'Whatcha gonna do, Boy?' Booty stirs.

'Shut up. Don't start,' I'm firin.

'Whatcha gonna do, *Kid Goanna*?' Booty smirks at Nevil.

'Nuthin, he doin nuthin! I'll get Kane, leave Nev outta it!' I stand up.

'No, I'll get Kane!' Big Boy thumps the table.

'Shut up, Boy.' I frown at him.

'No, you shut up, Mavis! I'll get Kane!' Gwen yells, suddenly coming alive.

'Are ya a man, Sonny Jim?' Booty laughs in Nevil's face.

'I'll kill that fucker!' Big Boy throws his fists in the air.

'No, no! I'll do it. I'll do it!' Gwen jumps up.

'Shut up n sit down, Mum, you talkin shit!' Big Boy growls.

'I'll do the bastard over. I did before!' I scream at all a them.

'Shut ya cake hole, Sister! You too, Gwenny. Let the boys here deal whit him!' Booty roars.

'I'm dealing with him!' The voice coming from the doorway echoes with violence. I swing about wildly. Standin there, shotgun in hand, killer look on her face is Missus Warby. Seventy years if she a day. Hair colour a frosty mornin. She feeble. The woman can like hardly get bout. But her eyes queer.

The woman looks like a maniac. Dressed from head to toe in black. Pair a man's boots on her feet. Man's big buckle belt slung offa hips. She lookin to kill. She looks small in her dead husband's clothes.

Everyone is speechless. Then Booty pulls himself up to his feet n says, 'Missus Warby, what the frig are you doin?'

She adjusts her hip belt and walks into the room. 'Never, never has anyone put anything past me in my life. I know now the real grief Kane has caused this fine woman before me. God has spoken to me, Mister Dooley, he has told me that the seeds of contempt, the seeds of hell are sown right here in Mandamooka! Right here in Mister Darryl Kane! He's killing folk with his business! That's right, murder! The man tries to set this woman and her little boy up for his own evil doings! *I won't stand for it!* It's always the old people, women and children to go first, isn't it? Yes, siree, always the weak ones to go down first.' She slides a shell into the shotgun chamber.

'Missus Warby, stop right now!' I jump to my feet. *The woman crazy-cracked. Yep, after all these years she done finally lost her poor ol scone. Ivy Warby a flat out lunatic. N she gonna do some damage.*

'Grieve no more, my good friend. I shall free you from the Devil's arms. Mister Kane has just crossed a river and he's got no chance of coming back. You could say he's stuck up a river of poop without a paddle.' She raises the gun in the air, eyes blazin as she runs her mole-flecked hand over the barrel.

I reel backwards. *The woman nutty as a fruit cake. Her red eyes done tell me that. She gone, long gone. The woman's mad. She finally cracked.*

Suddenly, from the corner a me eye, I see a small, fast movement, then like a bright flash somebody flies past me. I feel a breeze on me face. It happens so fast that I wonder if all this is real. *I wonder if me own head's bein so fucked whit I don't know shit from shampoo any more. Maybe it's me is goin round the bend? Maybe none a this is true. Could a woman be maginatin all a this?* I fall back gainst the table. The shotgun comes to life. The blast echoes loudly through the room. Me eardrums explode. Blood rushes to me head. *It's rainin? A woman feel rain peltin down her body.*

I look up. The ceiling starts crumblin. *Show's over. That's all she wrote.*

Someone's dead.

16

Hostage Taker

Trevor lies curled up on the floor, arms coverin his head. The boy whimpers like a gut-kicked dog. He in total fear.

Booty, grey-faced, stands by the fridge holdin onto Big Boy's shoulders. Big Boy looks ready to have a turn, his body all hunched over. He holds his hand up to his mouth like he gonna spew up.

Gwen crouches near the stove holdin a lump of wood in one hand, her dress tucked up into her bloomers as she stares fish-eyed round the kitchen.

On the other side of the room near the doorway lies Nevil, his arms wrapped round the laid-out figure of Missus Warby, the gun beside them.

Everything silent. Not one word, no one even breathin. The air stinks like gunpowder. In the distance I hear sirens – police, the ambulance.

I lift meself up from the table and walk over on shaky legs to the figures curled up on the floor. *They dead; me Nev, Missus Warby. There ain't no God in this world. Why would the woman take up arms? To kill people jus like that.*

A picture show flashes cross me eyes. I see me Nevie runnin cross the lawn, a football in his tiny, grubby hands. I see him sayin his first word: 'Mum'. Most of all I see Booty holdin him up on his shoulders like a trophy, tellin him he be a gooder footballer than any a em mugs on the field. His uncle loved him so much. Yep, he were like Booty's son. Now me boy gone. I hunch me shoulders forward as a scream rises in me throat.

Suddenly, Nevil's head rises up from Missus Warby's chest. 'Close shave, old girl.' He shakes her gently.

Missus Warby sits up, glancin round the room. 'What's wrong here?' She eyeballs each of us in turn. She look really stunned like. Her face white as a bleach-washed shirt.

Then like a red n white streak somebody bursts through the front door n tears round the room. The sirens grow louder.

'Nevil! My Nevil!' Gracie screams hysterically, her hands crossed on her chest, her mouth goin ten to the dozen.

'Gracie! Gracie, he's all right!' I grab her by the shoulders and shake her hard.

'Wha ...?' She turns and looks round at the mess. In the corner she spots Nevil and rushes at him. 'Gunfire? Who?' she asks.

'Accident,' Gwen says, pullin herself up from the woodheap.

Suddenly the sirens stop. I rush to the window. Lined from one end of the yard to the other are police cars. By the front gate the Mandamooka ambulance sits, doors open for business.

Hunched down, holdin a loudspeaker in one hand and a pistol in the other, is Max Brown. By his side are bout three or four other cops all armed to the teeth, pointin their weapons straight at me front door.

'Mavis Dooley,' the loudspeaker kicks into life. 'It's your friend Max Brown here. Can you hear me, Mave? Missus Dooley, let the hostages go. Let the hostages go.'

'Fucken hell! Fuck, fuck!' Gwen squeezes up beside me n takes a peek.

'Mavis, come out. Mavis, it's your old mate, Max Brown. Come on, Mave, make it easy on yourself.'

'What the bloody hell!' Missus Warby shoves her face at the window.

'Nevil! Nevil Dooley, are you in there son? Nevil, is anyone injured?' The loudspeaker blares.

'Oh shit! Oh shit! Missus Warby, I hate to talk to any woman like this but that was a fucken stupid thing to do!' Booty scolds.

The loudspeaker crackles. 'What do you want, Mavis? What are your demands?'

'Now listen here, Mister Dooley, there's no place for you to be swearing at me like that! He'll hear you, He will. God will strike you down, son!'

'Missus Warby, shut the fuck up!' Gwen turns on her.

'Is Nevil okay? Is anyone alive?' Max gets to his feet and moves towards the front door.

'Shut up! None a this would a happened if it hadn't

been for Gwen her lover boy!' I turn on Gwen, pokin a finger into her chest. 'That's right, Gwen, you n that piece a shit, Kane! Now look what ya both got a woman into, eh! I ain't a well woman, Gwen, whit me blood pressure n stuff. You'll all be the death of me!'

'Mum, shut up, don't you start,' Nevil yells, spit flyin from his gob.

'Listen here, Sonny Jim, don't you talk to ya mother like that!' Booty explodes.

'I'll kill that Edge, I promise ya that!' Big Boy lets it rip.

'Mavis Dooley, can you speak? I'll ring through on the phone. Pick the phone up when it rings! Mavis, can you hear me?'

I swing on Big Boy. 'Yeah, if it hadn't been for your mother none a this shit woulda happened. I don't blame you, son. Gwenny shoulda stayed away from Kane when I told her!'

'Jean Rhys! That's right, Nevil, you wantin to be a fucken woman is what set all the wheels runnin here,' Booty yells, the vein on his forehead throbbin. 'All this started from then! A man tried his heart out to set ya straight but, oh no, Nevil wanna be actin like a sheila!'

'Leave him alone, Mister Dooley, the boy's misled is all. Suffer the little children. I've known this boy here since he was this high.'

'Hey, anyone want a toke?' Gracie wanders round the room, joint in mouth, stubbie in hand.

'Mavis, pick the phone up! Nevil, son, pick up the phone! For God's sake pick up the phone!' Max Brown crackles into thin air. 'I'm here if you want to talk.'

'Never thought I'd see the day where me own mate would turn her back on me!' Gwen squeals.

'Anyone for a stubbie?'

'Missus Dooley, the police are out there.'

'Vengeance will be mine, yes sir. Some people in this town respect me and you know why? That's right, Mister Dooley, *because I care*! Never was the one to turn my back on others! I've been your sister's neighbour for years and it's my Christian duty to keep an eye on her and Nevil. When my husband passed on, who was there for me? Yes, that's right, Mavis and Nevil.'

'Missus Dooley, Missus Dooley.' Trevor shakes my elbow.

'Ohhh right, now don't you friggin start! Comin here fillin Nevil's head full a shit! Ya wrecked his life! Ya wrecked my life!' I push him backwards.

'The phone. Missus Dooley, the *phone*!'

'Jealous! Yeah, Mavis, ya jealous a me an Darryl!'

I turn on Gwen. 'Oh yeah, Gwen. Jealous my arse! I be lookin out for you n this is the thanks a woman gets! I done told ya Kane was nuthin but trouble. Ya wouldn't listen to me, would ya? Fine friend ya are sayin I is jealous. Ya talkin shit n ya know it.'

'Missus D, don't talk to my mother like that!' Big Boy comes at me, a scowl on his face.

'Any demands? Mavis Dooley, pick up the phone! Missus Mavis Dooley, pick up the phone, woman!' Max Brown shouts in the front yard.

'Missus Dooley, the phone's ringing. Shall I get it?'

'That's right, Trevor. This is why this all started – because of your fucken phone!'

'Mum, don't speak to my friend like that! There's no reason for it. Trevor's not brainwashing me, I'm my own person! Mum, I'm not a baby any more.'

'Mum, Mum Dooley, Max wants to talk to you on the phone,' Gracie says, pullin at my sleeve.

'You talk to him, Gracie!' I shout, then glare at Trevor. *The hide a it! Yeah, it all went downhill the day he turned up. My life was fine til all this shit started goin on. Now a woman got all this happenin round her. Trevor ain't made nuthin any easier for me, that's fer sure.*

'Now, dear, settle down. Want me to make you a nice cup a tea? Okay, come on, Nevil, come and help me round up some morning tea.' Missus Warby goes to the stove and puts the kettle on.

'A joint! You want me to provide you with drugs and beer? Mavis, what's going on there? Look, I'll send one of the boys down to get Doris from Legal Aid. I know what you've been through, you can talk to me, Mavis. Come on out Mavis, please!' Max's voice sounds desperate.

'Missus Dooley, *the police are speaking to you.* They're outside with guns! Look, look there! They have a sniper on Missus Warby's roof!' Trevor pushes me to the window.

I look out. *Bad business. Bad egg business. Guns pointin right at me window.* I feel me heart hammerin. The piss in me bowels is buildin up to pressure point. It don't look too good. Cops surroundin the joint like ants on a sugarbowl.

A woman's gonna be done over here any minute. Have to tell Max bout all this here, set him straight. He'll understand.

Out the corner a me eye I catch a glimpse of Gracie as like in slow motion, she bends down and picks up the shotgun. *The girl's eyes are outta it. She's high as a kite.*

All hell is gonna cut loose. Gracie, cops n guns not a real good mix. The cops are lookin in. They'll see everythin – they'll see how it look like Gracie linin up to shoot.

Before I can scream 'drop it', she brings the rifle up to her shoulder and points it straight at Missus Warby. 'Bang. Gotcha.' She laughs shrilly.

Me guts churn water. A psycho power tell me what gonna happen next. *Yep, everybody know the Queensland coppers gun happy. Cut ya down for any reason at all. Kill ya arse, specially if ya black. Right now they gonna see what they wanna. We don't stand a chance. We red-lined.*

Before a woman can shout a warnin, the window explodes, shatterin glass through the whole room. Everythin a roar, sorta like water peltin down a waterfall.

Here we go again. 'Down, get ya arses down!' I shout to the room.

I feel somethin pass me head n a *whhhiizzzz* sound. I feel me hair part as it whistle by, the cold breeze of a bullet.

Instinct drop me to the floor. Me head spinnin like a merry-go-round. Me eyes shootin colours like a fireworks. *This time someone gotta be hurt. This time somebody gotta be dead.*

Yep, ain't no cop fire off guns n miss their targets. The room's suddenly full a people. I hear boots chargin n stompin round the room. People yellin n screamin in all directions. I stare at the black-and-white lino on me floor. *It look dirty. A woman gotta get offa her big arse n clean it. Fat stains n scratches mark the little squares. Eh, there ya go, ya think ya kitchen's clean n spotless til ya really have a good eyeball at it. Hope no one ever noticed. Shamejob havin filthy lino. Course a woman could buy new stuff. Yep, the bingo money'd cover it.*

I let me thoughts go when I feel somethin hard jammed into the small a me back. A gun. A gun jammed into me spine. *Hope those bastards ain't got mud on their big useless boots. Cartin dirt onto a woman's already fucked-up lino.*

I search the room whit me eyes. *Who'd they get? Gracie? Is Gracie dead? Oh God, no, no! Please, God, don't let Gracie be dead.*

'Fucken pricks! Get off me fucken head! Get up!' Booty's voice screams loud and clear but full a fear.

'Help! Oh God! I'm innocent! It's all a terrible mistake! For God's sake, I'm Trevor Wren Davidson! Let me go! Oh Jesus … get that gun out of my face!' Trevor shouts real high, his voice bouncin off the walls.

'There ain't no Jean Rhys! I made her up! Yes, made it all up! I'm not fucken Edge! It's not what you think!' Nevil shouts.

'Get your filthy paws off me, son. Don't you dare

manhandle me! I'll notify Reverend Clinton of this, you hear me, Max Brown! You ought to be ashamed of yourself! And leave her alone! She's not one of your crooks! Get off Missus Dooley's back, you, you – you sinner!' Missus Warby shrieks.

'Darryl Kane is Isaac Edge. I'll tell you everything. Jean Rhys, yes, even about her,' Gwen yells at the top of her lungs.

'I had nuthin to do with it. I don't own a gun! It's hers, Missus Warby's, that old lunatic! Said she'd blow Darryl Kane away! The gun went off by accident! No one was gonna shoot at youse,' Big Boy sobs.

'Fucken freaky, man! Hey, Max, whatcha call that sorta weapon?' Gracie asks, gigglin.

I heave a deep sigh. *The girl alive.*

Somehow I'm hauled to me feet n marched out the front door whit the gun jammed in me kidneys. I silently curse Missus Warby to hell n back. A woman jus sick to death a the police station. I throw a glance over me shoulder n watch as everyone is dragged, pulled n shoved into the big mob a gungie cars linin the street.

Be frigged if a woman can go through any more a this shit. I wearin down fast. Can't hold up for too long now. I look out the rear window as the gungie car tears off down the street, the siren going fall bore. Yep, I'm fucked here now. They got me as some sorta hostage taker. Ah well, Mavis Dooley, ya time has finally come.

17

The Sun West of the Mountains

Darryl Kane, aka Isaac Edge, glares poison-eyed as the Ds march him past us. 'Bitch. Nearly had youse.' He wears a sour look of defeat and hate as he stares at me then Nevil.

'Now, Mister Edge, that's where you're wrong!' Missus Warby spits out, her face scarlet. 'The thing is, *I* almost had *you*! Yes, sir, you are a disease on this good community, and I won't tolerate people like you trying to hurt *children*! You see, I've known Nevie since this high.' She motions with one arm. 'You could say he's the son I never had. And if you think you'd have got away with all this, well, Mister Doodad, that's where you're mistaken!'

Gwen stands up, hands outstretched towards Kane as though the answer will float into her open palms. 'But why?' she croaks.

I watch the way her face collapses, like she gonna bawlbaby. I feel sorta bad for her. Another kick in the guts. *Yeah, well, this time least it ain't me.*

'Because of what *she* did!' Darryl swings round n glares at me whit hard green eyes. 'That black bitch made me look a fucking idiot! I never liked her from day one. I could of had you. You realise what you done to me! Wrecked my life! You made a fuckhead of me in front of the entire town, then my wife pissed off on me after you had to open that filthy trap of yours! I'll be back – and when I do I'll be chasing you down, woman!' Spit flies from his mouth, he shakes handcuffed fists at me.

'Darryl, it ain't ever had anythin to do whit me. If you the big man ya wouldna tried to kick Gwen in the guts when she were down. As for Samantha, well, good job, pity the girl didn't piss off on ya a long time ago. Chase me down, eh – good luck, cos I be here n ya knowin where I live. Alls I can say is have a nice holiday in the *big joint*.' I give him a bright smile. *There, take that, Mister Smartarse!*

Suddenly he lunges, his handcuffed hands tryin to grab hold a me. I step back and fall against the wall.

'Back! Back, Kane. Settle down!' The fat D grabs him by the arm and holds him tightly to the spot.

'You did all this to Mavis and Nevil because she sat on you at the pub? Ya gotta be joking!' Gwen looks at him. I read the woman's face – he's a fucken lunatic, it suggests.

'She wrecked my marriage and my life. Everyone heard what she said to Samantha at the pub. Sam just couldn't take it. For fuck's sake! The woman took away my life!'

Max gives Kane the once over, his lips curled back like somewhere's a bad smell. 'Well, mate, I'm surprised Samantha didn't leave you years ago.'

'But,' Gwen frowns at Darryl, 'Where the hell did this *Jean* woman come into it?'

The skinny D taps Darryl on the shoulder. 'Yeah, come on now Kane, why don't you tell us the truth? It makes no sense at all.'

Darryl turns to Gwen, an oily smirk on his dial. 'That's the good part.' He looks around at us. 'It was Dotty Reedman who told me about this sheila Jean Rhys staying at Dooley's. Yeah, me and Dotty are real good mates if you know what I mean.' He grins, runnin a hand through greasy, slicked back hair. 'I knew I could set it all up. Things started to get a bit hot for me with the Bullya cops, I needed to throw the scent another way.' He stops for a second and tucks his navy singlet into his arse-tight jeans. 'I knew I could kill three birds with one stone. I decided to throw the scent that way!' He jabs a finger at me n Nevil.

'But ...' Gwen begins.

'Come on, Edge, time to move on.' The fat detective grabs him by the singlet and pushes him down the hall, Darryl makes a wild U-turn and swings about to face us. 'I'll be back!' he shouts, his eyes poppin from his head n his face bloated and red with anger. 'And if it's the last thing I ever do, I'm gonna get you, Mavis Dooley!'

As the detective swings him back round he cries out over his shoulder. 'I love you, Gwenny!'

'Well, I don't love you! Ya wanka!' Gwen shouts back.

'See you in hell, Kane!' Missus Warby throws her partin shot, eyes ablaze.

Max Brown motions Missus Warby to step forward. The man looks tongue-tied. 'I'm charging you with possessing an unregistered firearm. Now, look, I don't want any objections or threats, Missus Warby, please.'

Missus Warby pulls herself up, her spine ruler-straight. 'The Reverend will know. That's right, Max, Reverend Clinton will hear about this! If it weren't for me that Edge, Kane, whoever on God's earth he is, would have got away with all this! I'm just doing my duty as a good citizen of this town.' She bends forward. 'I expect you to overlook this little error.' She smiles, then bangs a hand down on the counter. 'It'd be the best thing for you. After all, I was the one that brought Kane undone, wasn't I?'

Max looks past Missus Warby. 'Mavis, are you okay?'

'Yeah, I'll live,' I tell him, shruggin my shoulders.

Max sighs, offerin us a tired look. 'It's over now. I think everyone can go home. But you must all understand I've only done what's required of me.'

'Max, how'd you know about the gun?' Booty questions, gettin to his feet.

'Missus Fellows from across the road rang in, saying that Mavis Dooley had finally cracked. She heard the gun go off and reckoned that, you know … you were all dead.' Max smiles thinly.

'So, Darryl is the Edge? I mean, I sorta sussed somethin wrong whit him. All those phone calls to Bullya. I jus couldn't be too sure though. Til Mavis tipped me off.' Gwen stares past us, confused.

'Yep, reckon we definitely got our man this time. No mistake – but, Gwen, who is Jean?'

'Long story, I reckon.' Gwen laughs.

'She never was here, Max. She gammon, a ghost,' I say.

'Mavis, where did all this begin?'

'When Nevil woke up one day,' I answer, not willin to say more.

A woman don't wanna be raisin the dead again.

'Put it this way, I don't think you'll hear about her ever again. That's unless you happen to read her books,' Trevor butts in, giving Nevil a mysterious wink.

'Yes, well, that's good because I'm sick of hearing that name!' Max laughs, he motions to the door. 'You're all free to go.'

The street is quiet n dead. I look across to Missus Warby's but there's no movements there. *The poor ol bag, probly plottin for the next show!* I turn away from the broken window, put the kettle on and sit down. 'Nevil, the big game's on tamarra, what ya gonna do?'

'I'm playing, Ma,' he answers with a cheeky grin.

I peer at him. 'Nevil – you really are Nevil, aren't ya?'

'Yep, Nevil Dooley, male, twenty-one years old,' he answers with a glint in his eyes.

'But ...?' I turn to Trevor.

'Missus Dooley, I'm not who you think. I, well, I'm not a painter, a dancer or any of those things. I'm from The Crossroads publishing house. I'm here to – well, to help this genius!' He laughs and throws Nevil a look of real respect.

'Oh yeah?' I don't understand. *Publishin? What the hell he on bout?*

'You see, Nevil is a gifted writer. That's right, Nevil has a massive artistic talent. He's been writing for some time now. Missus Dooley, Nevil is an artist.'

'Writing! Writing! Okay, come on, no more jokes. I'm sick to death a all this shit!'

'No, Missus Dooley, I'm absolutely serious.'

'Mum, what you gotta understand is this, I couldn't tell you … because …'

'Because he was ashamed. That's right, Missus Dooley, *ashamed* of his own talent! I first heard of Nevil's incredible ability through another friend of mine, Glenda Winterson, a creative writing instructor from Bullya. Nevil is still working on his novel. It's called *The Sun West of the Mountains*. Glenda convinced Nevil to send me the manuscript, which he did. It was brilliant, I loved it! When I met him in Bullya he told me where he was from and what sort of life he had. The thing is, he guessed no one would ever believe he could write such a book; and of course he was right. But how could he go on living here and discover his true potential? Explore his feminine side? That's right, Missus Dooley – his novel is being written through the eyes of a female protagonist.'

I gawk at them, me gob falls onto me chest. *It's like some crazy-cracked maginin. Me Nevil a writer!*

'So, in order to really go there, I decided I had to be Jean Rhys. Don't worry, Ma, there's nothing suss in it. She's my favourite author; she wrote *Wide Sargasso Sea*. She was ahead of her time; she wrote about society's underdogs; about rejection and the madness of isolation. I know it sounds all crazy to you, Ma, but this is about who *I* am. Being Nevil Dooley in this town is a challenge.' Nevil stops, runs a hand cross his brow then continues, 'That's right, Ma, I was never the person everyone thought I was. Cos what choices did I have? Disappoint you, Uncle Booty, me mates? I knew the risk in doing what I did.' He looks me in the eye. 'Ma, a lot of people would never understand me and they wouldn't want to. What choices does a black fella have in this town except football? None unless ...' He goes quiet.

Trevor smiles back fondly. 'Unless you took that one slim chance, which you did!'

'Why couldn't you tell me? Why go to all this shitty trouble pretendin to be a sheila! Ya coulda told us! It's mad! The trouble we all went through, Nevil!' I force out the words, me eyes achin, me teeth chatterin. *The boy felt he couldn't tell his own mumma. What, I'm a monster? All this fuckery for nuthin.*

'Not meaning to hurt your feelings, Ma, but I knew you'd never understand my being passionate about something you never experienced yourself. About writing and getting into someone's head. You couldn't help me, Ma. I was on my own and it was exciting! I needed to be a woman here in this town! I needed to be so obviously different. Yeah, I wanted all those reactions ... I didn't mean for you to feel—'

'Let down,' Trevor throws in.

'But, Nevil, ya coulda guessed the way people would be! Ya knowed they would jus think ya gone in the head. Everybody know ya ain't no woman! Ya already knowed what it's like to be different! Why couldn't ya just magine ya Jean?'

'No, I actually wanted to look and feel the way a woman does. Ma, I know what it's like to be treated different but that difference is based on skin colour, not my gender. I couldn't go away someplace else and do this – that would be defying the whole purpose of what I set out to do. I wanted those reactions! Yeah, of course everyone knows I'm a man. I wanted to gauge their emotions to all this.'

'To have people look at him with another perspective. It's, um, like a huge experiment.' Trevor smiles. 'No, I didn't have anything to do with it, Missus Dooley, it was all Nevil's idea.'

'To get ya guts kicked in by the town? To be called faggot n whatever else? It don't make right sense to me. This book? What? Is it worth all the trouble, Nevil?'

'Sorry I put you through all of this Mum. But, yes, it is worth all the trouble. The reactions from everyone – including you and Uncle Booty – were priceless.'

'But all the grief for us!'

'I figured you'd handle it, Mum. Ya made of sterner

stuff. But it all started to go wrong with this drug business. I hadn't planned on being dragged off by the gungies ...' His voice gets all excited now. 'Anyway, this book is about a woman called Lucinda Lawrey. She's my hero. Um, she's a thirty-something female, living in the bush, and struggling to make ends meet after her husband ups and leaves her. Naturally, she's shattered and tries to rebuild her life in a town that's hell-bent on destroying her with gossip and treachery – sort of Mandamooka. And, yes, she's different, she has a high IQ, loves Tolstoy and surrealist art. Lucinda bucks against the stereotypes. Writing about her is my heart and soul!'

The boy is so soft. Yep, was always the first one to cry at sad movies n stuff. He deep as the ocean. But I don't really sussin what he on bout. Not all a it.

'Gee, son, I never knew.' *I can't say anythin.* I stop and stare back at this stranger, this stranger I gave birth to. *What can a woman say?*

'Why? Why write as a woman?' I ask reachin in the cupboard for some Tim Tams. *A woman sure need calmin.*

'Because I can, because of the perspective thing, because I think it's easier to be a man in this sort of place than to be a woman. A woman's got to be as tough as a man, but not show it. And if she does, she's an outcast. Lucinda's different – not just by being bright and independent – but she's black and she's seeking a better life for herself and her kids. That's what the book's really about – Lucinda searching for a way to escape the constrictions of *her* town.' Nev's voice is close-to-teary.

'Nevie? Don't cry, son.' I go round and cuddle him. *Was always a good boy me Nevil. Always looked after his mumma.*

'You've done a fine job, Missus Dooley. But I think that's the problem with some small towns, they crush people like Nevil. Bend, twist and pulp those who are different. Dissecting each other and criticising the world, all behind that facade of sincerity, yes, and all the while knowing what they are doing, but not caring. It's as though the world they inhabit stops and begins right here in Mandamooka. I suppose it's that visible difference they can't handle – the physical difference of someone is a threat to them, like Nevil. I think that's the sum of it, don't you?' Trevor sits back in the chair, tired like.

'Like a chain. Always said this town is like a chain round your neck. Nevil, ya know, Lucinda's life sounds like yours. Could it be that ya writin bout yerself, son?' I look across at a them. 'And what's gonna happen now? I mean bout the book?'

'Yeah, it's sort of autobiographical. But mostly it's fiction. And Trevor's here to help me with the rest of it.'

'Yep, to help Nevil knock it into shape. It's called editing. All those times you never saw us we were actually in Nevil's bedroom reworking the manuscript. I'm what you call an editor. Oh, and I also paint things in my spare time. So it wasn't all lies.'

'When the book's tidied up, Trevor's going to publish it,' Nevil says, scratchin his stubbled chin.

'So, you'll be famous? Fancy that, me boy a famous writer! Deadly!'

'Oh yes, he will be famous! See, the thing is this. Nevil being Aboriginal to start with and from the bush, where sport is the measure of manly talent – then his writing a first novel, and so brilliant, so achieved. He's created a unique character with Lucinda.'

'He has?' Gracie asks, walkin into the room with a scowl.

'Hello, Gracie. How are you, girl?' Nevil asks, standin up, openin his arms wide.

'Well, I've come here to tell you all some news. I'm leavin this dump. That's right, I'm burnin rubber outta here! Nevil, I can't live the way everybody else does round here. I come to say goodbye to you all.' Tears gather in her eyes.

'What about Nevil?' I ask.

'Well, I think Nev'll be goin his own way from now. I, um, wish youse well, Nevil. Hope everythin turns out for you. I'm off to Bullya. Got mesself some marches to go to.' She walks to the door. 'Oh yeah, one more thing! Hope Jean makes you happy! Cos from now I'm being like you, Nevil, tryin to make some sorta difference in this screwed up world.'

'Follow ya dreams, Gracie, cos when it comes down to it that's all ya got in the end. And promise ol Mum you'll come back n visit.' I stand to me tired legs n put me arms round her. 'Live ya dreams Gracie,' I say, real close.

'I know, Mum. I'll do that just for you.' And she walks out the door, passin Booty on her way.

'He back,' she tells him, throwin a thumb over her shoulder towards Nevil.

'Well, I'll be dammed! Gracie, before ya go, do somethin for this ol man here, eh. Keep ya nose clean.' Booty smiles at her.

'Count on it, man.' She giggles as she leaves.

Booty comes into the kitchen. 'What's going on here? What the fuck are youse up to now?' He looks at Nevil then Trevor.

'Don't ask, Brother, you'd never understand!' I laugh, pullin the fridge open and takin out a stubbie. 'Here, Bro, have a drink whit ya ol sister. Here's to Lucinda Lawrey! To Gracie Marley n to me boy!' I hold the stubbie in the air.

'Who the fuck is Lucinda? Ooohhh nooooo, don't tell me – it's him, right?' Booty glares at Nevil.

'That's where ya wrong, Brother!' *Yep, a woman feelin pretty solid. Lookandsee!* 'Here boys, have a celebration drink whit me.' I push the stubbies cross the table.

Booty throws me a look a surprise, then quick as he is, says, 'Well, I'll say one thing and that's I'll be fucked if a man can ever handle another Jean Rhys.' Then he roars whit laughter.

'Here's to Lucinda Lawrey!' we chorus, laughin up big.

I sit back n eyeball Nevil's face. *All these years he been shyin hisself away. Like a little kid whit a lollipop, leavin the best part for last. I wonder how I'll get on whitout him here. Cos sure as shit he'll be outta this town soon nough. That much a woman knows. Oh well, lookandsee. Tamarra's another day. Good things happen all a time to people anywhere. Why not to me?*

18

The Game

The announcer shouts into the microphone. 'Nevil Dooley has the ball! The kid from Mandamooka! He's going to make it! Oh no, Mad Dog takes him down!'

I turn to Gwen and Terry. 'Solid, eh?'

'Speaking of solid. Look over there, Mave,' Gwen says, pointin cross the field.

I glance cross the dusty expanse. Me gut drops. I throw a quick glance towards Terry.

He don't see her, good.

Dotty Reedman stands at the sidelines, holdin a box a oranges. The woman look like sheep fancied up as mutton.

She's got a pink n blue mini dress on – it rides up the woman's thighs like a sly hand crawlin up a leg. Her t-shirt is white, clingin to her hooters like glue to a piece a paper, showin her nipples. She got the hide to wear em bobby socks whit a pair a white sandshoes. She looks for all the world like the oldest woman cheerleader ever lived whit a face made up like ten picnics at a Sunday barbie. She all reds, blues, pinks, coloured up like to press somebody, to haul Terry's arse her way! *Yeah, she just don't give up. Like a dog whit a bone.*

'Go, Jerry! Go, son!' she yells, jumpin up n down on the spot.

I curl me mouth back, snarlin across at her. *She big-notin herself as usual. Yeah, who she think she is.*

'Go, Nev! Get the ball, son!' I yell, walkin closer to the sidelines.

'The ball, Jerry!' she yells louder when she look across and see me.

'Go, Nevil!' I bust a gut. *Yeah, me boy the best player for sure.*

White-hot, the announcer calls the game. 'Young Dooley has the ball. Look at him. Fast? He's like bloody lightning! He sidesteps Dougald Malley from the Rammers! Big Boy Hinch tears up the sideline and look at that boy run! Dooley passes the ball to Hinch. Hinch passes to Grunta. Grunta passes to Dooley!'

'Score! A score, Nev!' I look straight across at Dotty.

'The ball, Jerry! Get the frigging ball!' Dotty screams, her face blood-bright red.

'Young Dooley's pelting through them! Look at that! He's going to score! Nevil Dooley's going to score! Looks like the Blackouts might have the first point here today, folks!'

'After him! Up the side! Jerry, get your fat useless arse moving!'

'Keep goin, Nev!'

'He's scored! Mandamooka scores the first point!

Young Dooley does it again this year!'

'Pull up your act, Jerry! Faster, son, faster!' Dotty yells with fury.

'She nutty,' Gwen says, comin to stand beside me.

'The woman's a maniac.' Terry shakes his head, screwin up his eyes to peer across at her.

'Thought you liked her?' Gwen sneers.

'Yeah, as if! She not my type a woman, Gwenny. I like em like my tea, strong n black.' He laughs, throwin a particular look my way.

'Huh, coulda fooled me.' I give him a sour grin.

'Hey, Mave, is that who I think it is?' Gwen nudges me in the ribs and nods towards the other end of the field.

Missus Warby, eye spotters hangin from her neck, Akubra jammed on her head and wavin a Blackouts banner, sits on an esky, watchin Nevil's form like an eagle bout to swoop a rabbit.

'The Blackouts!' she screams for all it's worth, wavin her banner like a weapon at the Rammers. 'Go, Nev!'

I smile. *Wonder if she armed? If she gonna do the Rammers over. Ha, ha, har. Lookandsee!* I turn from her and watch as the Blackouts pelt down the field. Me eyes start to water when I spot Mad Dog chasin after Nevil like a bat outta hell. *His face look like a bad plum. All purplish n squashed in whit juice slidin down the side a it. Mad Dog got a score to settle whit Nevil. Nevil sure jammed him there that day at the shed. Boxed his arse! Seem like he ain't forgot either, he closin in on Nevil like one of Booty's pig dogs on a pig.* I groan in me guts. *Bad move, son.*

Nevil tears up the sideline, movin like a little bantam rooster. Sweat pours down his face, his legs pumpin as he flies past Jerry Reedman.

'Move in! Move in, Sonny Jim!' I turn to the loud voice comin from behind. Booty stands there, gut hangin out his singlet, a stubbie in one hand. Beside him, barkin, howlin and growlin are the pig dogs. *The man smell worser n a beer keg. He drunker n I ever seed him. Shamejob turnin up on Nevie's big day like that! I could hit the man in the head. Knock some sense into him!* I let the thought go and concentrate on the game.

Mad Dog motors down the field right behind Nevil. Mad Dog's fast, nearly fast as Nevil. I see it like slow motion as Mad Dog leaps through the air, a dirty smile on his dial as he lands full force on Nevil. *Wwwhhhuuummmmpppttthh!*

Nevil hits the dirt like a sack a potatoes. Red dust billows up to cloud round them. Mad Dog got him.

'Off! Get off, you fucka!' Booty roars, as the dust dances off to show the scufflin, grapplin forms of Nevil n Mad Dog in the dirt. Mad Dog got Nevil's face jammed right into the ground, holdin the back of his head and thumpin it up n down.

Before me legs can move, Booty gallops cross the field, the dogs barkin at his heels. He look for all the world like a big fat lizard scurryin cross the hot day. Me mouth opens but nothin comes out. Me ears roar. Me heart trips over.

Booty grabs the back a Mad Dog's jersey and lifts

him to his feet. Nevil jumps up, yellin n screamin at Booty.

Missus Warby scurries onto the field. 'Cheats! The Rammers are cheats!' she screams.

Suddenly Dotty Reedman charges towards Nevil. 'Bloody idiot! Can't play to save yourself!' She shoves Nevil in the chest.

That's it. I stand frozen to the spot as the mob, like drought stricken cattle pushin at water, crowd the field n start knucklin on.

I eyeball the field. *Always the way, yep, every year there's a blue. Maybe ol Bro shoulda set up his boxin ring here. Har, har, that'd be a fuckery riot, eh.*

The announcer kicks into life. 'No! No! Not again! Someone get those people off the bloody field!'

I watch as Max Brown tries to calm the wild crowd. *It's too much. A woman just ain't got the nerves to take it any more.* Then, as I head towards Dotty I spot Terry Thompson yellin at her.

He look angered up. His face all twisted n outta shape. Dotty just looks at him like he a Loony Tunes or somethin. 'Yes, well, I don't like you either!' she screams back at him.

Yep, saves me doin it! I hold in a deep, satisfied laugh. *Gotcha, Dotty! Yep, what ya put out ya get back.*

'The Blackouts take out this year's game!' the announcer belts out. 'And by the look of it I'd say there'll be some hard celebrating tonight. Maybe next year, Rammers. No doubt young Dooley's feeling proud of himself at this moment. Congratulations to the Blackouts!'

I look round at everyone. Me eyes can't see nuthin worth lookin at. Then Trevor comes into view. 'Coming home?' he asks, with a cheeky smile.

Nevil walks away from the squabblin mass and comes over to us. 'Last game ever.'

'Yep, well, ya gotta do whatcha gotta do.' A smile splittin me face.

Terry sidles over. 'You all comin over to my place for a barbie, Jean?' He throws the question at Nevil whit a wicked smile.

'Yep, reckon we need a bit a quiet. A woman feelin mighty runned down,' I answer.

Terry takes me hand as we walk outta the football grounds. *Giddy up! Dreams do come true.*

'By the way, Terry. It's not Jean any more. It's Lucinda!' Nevil pokes a finger in his chest and laughs cheekily.

So Jean Rhys departs and in her place is another woman. A woman I like.

A woman I know.